savior

EDEN SUMMERS

1
———

PENNY

I BURROW DEEPER UNDER THE COVERS, COCOONED IN luxurious silken sheets, nestled amongst extravagance.

I'm not ready to let go of sleep just yet. My mind still straddles the line of consciousness where the freedom of dreams overwhelms reality.

It's nice here.

Peaceful.

There's nothing but me and my imagination.

I fantasize about dragging my toes through the waves crashing against the shore in the distance. Raising my face to the sun. Swimming through crystal-clear water. I picture smiling faces beaming at me with gentle affection.

I visualize love.

"Good morning, my pretty Penny."

I freeze, my breath catching at the deep voice breeching my mental sanctuary.

The whiplash from dream to nightmare is harsh. Sickening. I panic, like always, then force myself to calm despite the lingering threat.

The owner of that voice is the devil.

He's the cause of my waking hell—a man without conscience or soul.

He's also the owner of this bed, and everything in it.

"It's time to get up." He tugs at the covers, dragging the material down to expose my face... shoulders... breasts.

I measure my breathing, not showing an ounce of emotion as he peers down at my naked body with a leering smile.

I'd prayed I wouldn't have to see him today. I'd begged, wished, and hoped he wouldn't return after he'd brutalized me last night, then left the house under the cover of darkness to undoubtedly destroy more lives.

I could've fled to my room with his disappearance. I should've escaped to my own bed instead of fearing a reprimand for leaving before I was dismissed.

But my prayers went unanswered.

They always do.

God can't help me here. Nobody can. I can't even help myself. Not against a heartless human trafficker such as the untouchable Luther Torian.

He scours my body with his gaze, trying to provoke me with the hunger in his eyes.

"Did you sleep well?" He drags the covers farther, along my stomach... pussy... thighs... all the way to my feet, exposing every inch of me in a deliberate incremental humiliation.

"Yes." I spare him the solitary syllable, giving the bare minimum of what he requires before I slide from the mattress, ignoring the lingering aches and pains born from his night of amusement.

"Did you dream of me?" he drawls.

I ignore the question and stare at the door, waiting for his freeing words of dismissal. He wants me to bite back—to snap—and I'm not going to give him the satisfaction.

Last night, he took what he needed. He devoured my aggressive fight along with my screams. Today, routine would suggest I'm meant to be allowed to rest.

"I said, did you dream of me?" He lashes out, grabs a fistful of my hair, and drags me toward him until I stumble into his tailored-suit covered chest.

My scalp screams in protest but I keep my lips pressed closed, my blood pounding through my veins as I clench my teeth and ignore the cloying need to scream for help.

His smile remains in place while his hold tightens. Always taunting. Always tormenting.

I blink slowly, remembering the one beautiful moment long ago when I responded to his devilry by spitting in his face. He'd balked. Stared. Snarled. His shock at my stupidity had been a reward, at least for a few brief seconds until reality set in and clenched fists rained down on me.

I used to lash out freely. I tried to deny him my humiliation whenever possible, yet he always claimed it more tightly in the aftermath.

Now I've come to realize I can manipulate him if my aggression is tactical. I only bite when I know it will work in my favor. I snap in the moments when I'm well aware he's going to violate me. I save all my fight for those moments *not* because his abuse still scares me after all these years, but because aggression is my only defense.

I scream and kick to excite him. To quicken his climax.

I bite and punch and thrash because my hostility is the only thing saving me from a far worse fate.

Now isn't one of those times, though. Not when he had me less than eight hours ago. Luther Torian is becoming an old man. I'm told he's already a grandfather. If I trigger any sort of a thrill the resulting perversion will take longer to conclude.

So I clench my teeth. Breathe deep. Force calm. And don't give him one fucking glimmer of what he wants.

"No." I hold my chin high. "I didn't dream of you."

His laugh lines deepen. "This is why you're my favorite, pretty Penny. You cling tight to your anger. It's invigorating."

He's right. I cling so tight.

Anger is all I have.

I hoard the emotion deep in my chest, using it as armor. I rarely show my fear anymore and never, ever weakness. I stopped giving him insight to those parts of me long ago, back when I figured out he detests fragility.

What he enjoys is the battle.

It's what he craves.

And as much as I hate to hand him his filthy perversions on a silver platter, it's far better to live under his roof than inside the haunted walls of the place where he houses the majority of his sex slaves.

Here, in his Greek Island mansion, I'm only forced to do unimaginable things once or twice a week.

If I was sent to live with his less fortunate captives, I'm led to believe I'd have to perform once or twice an hour. The beating and torture would be unending instead of intermittent.

Permanent, not cyclic.

He releases my hair and grips my chin, his fingers digging into skin. "Don't worry. One day I'll grow tired of you."

I swallow, the deep chill of fear increasing.

It's such a twisted, nauseating reality to want to be here. To fight to remain under this roof where I have clean sheets and a comfortable bed. I've made friendships in this gilded cage. I have relative freedom.

I'll do anything—*give* anything—to remain as far as possible from the revolving door of Luther's personal harem. And so far, my tactics have worked. I'm the longest-standing woman in residence, having seen innumerable victims—*sisters*—come and go during my time.

I can't lose my position.

I'll never survive if I'm forced to leave.

"Go." He shoves me backward, chin first. "Make yourself look pretty. We're going to have visitors soon."

I stumble, quickly righting myself, the voice of curiosity tingling at the tip of my tongue.

Visitors are never a good thing. New faces mean new perversions. Fresh instruments of torture.

"I'll make sure I'm at my best." I turn and walk for the door, my stride confident before I grab the handle and twist.

I should be relieved to have survived another night in his bed. But that emotion is never present. Not when I'm dead inside.

No, not dead.

Death would be a blessing. Pure nirvana.

Instead, I'm constantly plagued by life. Every breath is a punishment.

I step into the hall, my anger spiking when I see Robert

standing in wait, his back against the wall, his mouth curved in a sickening grin.

"Afternoon." He licks his lips, his gaze riveted on my bare chest. "Did you have a good night?"

I maneuver around him, determined not to engage.

"It sounded like you were enjoying yourself." He pushes off the wall and follows after me, his bulky frame hovering close at my back, raising the hair on my neck. "You know your screams make me hard."

I keep walking, keep eating up the distance to my room.

"How does it feel knowing you'll soon be mine?" he taunts.

I stop, not just my steps, but my breathing.

"You heard right." There's humor in his voice. "Luther agreed to hand you over once he's finished with you. Isn't it a relief to find out you'll be saved from the whorehouse yet again?"

Everything kicks back in—my fractured heartbeats, my panicked speculation, and so much stifling anger. It takes all my strength not to let my emotions show.

Luther is a monster. Always has been. Always will be. But Robert's violations will be an even deeper layer of hell seeing as though I've been an untouchable temptation to him for so long.

I raise my chin. Square my shoulders. "I look forward to our time together." I don't wait for a reply. My numb feet carry me along the hall, his laughter haunting me as he leaves in the opposite direction.

When I reach the door to my shared bedroom, the slightest sense of relief warms my chest until quickened footsteps carry from the kitchen.

"Penny, wait." Tobias, Luther's son, runs along the hall, his tiny frame barreling toward me.

I force a smile. I force so much fake bravado for this boy that it physically pains me. "Hey, little man. What are you up to this morning?"

He beams up at me, not acknowledging my nudity or the myriad of new bruises and scratches now marking my skin.

The sight before him is normal. The brutality an everyday occurrence. This beautiful little boy, with his sleek black hair and his deep blue eyes, is immune to the horrors surrounding him.

"I finished the writing task you gave me."

"Already?" I ruffle his hair. "That was fast."

"I've been awake forever. Dad took me out last night to meet my brother and when we returned I couldn't sleep."

Unease slithers down my spine. "Your brother?"

"Half-brother," he corrects. "His name is Cole. He's big and scary-looking. He's really old, too. Even older than you. But Dad says we have a lot in common."

I fake a chuckle, the sound bubbling over the bile rising in my throat.

I knew Luther had an adult son. Some of the women I've met in here have told stories about him. The kind of Chinese whispers capable of making my skin crawl. They spoke of his reputation in Oregon. About him being a well-known criminal. A *murderer*. And also the apple of his father's eye.

I've just never known him to come to the Greek Islands. Not once in the lifetime I've been here.

"I'm not *really* old, Tobias." But I am *really* worried.

Luther's son has to be the visitor. "And I'm sure your brother isn't either."

He shakes his head. "That's not what I want to talk to you about. I have to show you my assignment. It's really good."

My heart squeezes at his innocence. "You can show it to me later. Let me get dressed first."

His face falls. "Please?"

"Later." I ruffle his hair again. I have to speak to the other women and warn them of the approaching danger. "I promise."

He pouts and blinks those puppy-dog eyes at me. "Please. Please. *Please*."

This time my chuckle isn't forced, only short-lived. "Later, gorgeous boy."

"Fine." His shoulders slump as he huffs and storms off in the direction he came.

I wait a pain-filled heartbeat, making sure he's out of sight before I rush into my room.

It's exactly how it is every day—three sets of bunk beds evenly spaced along the side wall. Five beds are perfectly made, with the lower bed in the middle bunk being the anomaly.

Lilly is still under the covers, curled in a ball, her gaze meeting mine. Those soul-shattered eyes are the only reason I don't blurt out the news about Luther's son.

This woman—this *girl*—is close to breaking under the pressure of our tortured existence.

She rarely leaves our small sanctuary, choosing to sleep away the nightmares as much as possible. There's no fight left in her. No life. It's only a matter of time before she slips through the revolving door.

"Morning, Lill." I continue to the closet, pull out a loose sundress, and slide it over my head, letting the thin cotton cover the bruises on my thighs and hips.

She watches me, her eyes dreary, her skin ashen. "Luther's son is coming."

I wince and walk toward her, climbing onto her bed to spoon under the covers. "Did you hear me talking to Tobias?"

"No," she whispers. "Chloe told me. It's all I can think about."

I relax a little, entirely selfish with relief at not having been the bearer of bad news. "How did she find out?"

"She overheard Robert and Chris talking." She sucks in a shaky breath. "It's a business meeting. She thinks he's going to help traffic more women."

I wrap my arm around her waist and hug her tight. "Lill, I need you to listen to me. I know you're scared, but you can't keep hiding in here. Luther loathes fragility. You have to find something to fight for. You can't give up, especially if his son is coming. You need to be strong."

"I can't." Her voice breaks. "I don't know how."

An ache forms under my sternum, the discomfort building.

She's going to be taken away. I've seen it happen too many times not to predict the separation.

"All I can think about is my family, which only makes me want to cry." She turns into me, her face pressing against my shoulder, her tears heating my skin. "I miss them, Penny. I just want to go home."

I hug her tighter and press my eyes closed, knowing exactly how hard it is to get out of the emotional mine-field. "You need to forget your past. You can't think of anything before your time here. It doesn't exist. Not anymore."

A sob escapes her. "I don't know how you stay strong."

"There's no choice. We both know the alternative is worse."

If there was another option to combat my reality, I'd take it. But I've learned the ways of Luther's world. There's no escape. Only darker pits of despair if we don't comply.

I can't kill him. I wouldn't dare to try. Not when failure would turn this nightmare into something unimaginable.

Women have attempted before and the aftermath still haunts me.

One woman even came close to success. Cody. A victim barely in her twenties.

She'd been frail. Mindless. And didn't think of the consequences of stealing a visitor's gun before she aimed the barrel at Luther.

She also didn't anticipate the gun's safety lock or know how to switch it off after she failed to successfully pull the trigger.

Cody went from elation to annihilation in the space of heartbeats. But not through physical pain. At least not to start with. After Robert and Chris tackled her to the ground, Luther told them to fetch another one of the women from his personal harem—her closest confidant.

He'd then enlightened both women on how to turn off the gun's safety and held Cody's trembling hands steady as they found a new aim for the barrel.

He'd ripped out her heart with the pull of a trigger. He made her murder a woman she loved.

Then he tied her, face down, to the dining table,

allowing anyone and everyone who walked into his home the chance to fulfil their perverted fantasies for days on end before he sent her through his revolving door.

"You haven't always been this way, have you?" Lilly whispers. "I've heard stories."

I stiffen, well aware of the tale she's referring to. The one where I foolishly thought my tactics were far better than anyone else's.

"It's been a long time since Luther has seen any weakness from me."

She pulls back to look at me with tear-soaked eyes. "But you—"

"Yes, I tried to kill myself. But that was out of strength, not instability."

It was how I planned to win this game.

A final *fuck you.*

All it took was a hair-dryer and a warm, soothing bath.

I don't even remember what it felt like. The electrocution. The death. One second, I was lying in the scented water. The next, I opened my eyes to Robert's angry face looming over me as he paused chest compressions while I lay on the chilling wet tiles of the bathroom floor.

"Did Luther go easier on you afterward?"

"No. It never gets easier. You need to remember that."

"Then how did you survive?" She punishes me with her sorrow. Kills me with her pained tone. "How could you...?"

I shrug. "Luther gave me no choice."

He kept me on a leash for weeks, dragging me everywhere he went. There was no reprieve from his horror. No respite from the constant onslaught of mental and physical torture. "But right now, you have a choice, Lill. You can either give him exactly what he wants or you'll be sent some place far worse than this."

Her lips tremble as her tears fall. "I'm not strong like you."

"You are. You have to be."

She sniffs and nuzzles back into my shoulder as heavy footfalls approach along the hall.

There's more than one set, the deep pound resembling a pack of men.

Robert, Luther, and Chris pass the open doorway, not glancing in our direction before they continue out of sight, the front door slamming shut moments later.

"They must be going to get Luther's son." I kiss her forehead and slide from the bed. "We need to get ready."

She doesn't budge. It's clear she doesn't have the strength to appease Luther's depraved fantasies, and my heart breaks at the imminent goodbye. She might last another week. Maybe a few days.

"Come on, Lill. Get dressed. Do your hair. It's better to fly under the radar than draw attention by being unprepared."

She sinks farther under the covers. "In a minute."

The ache in my chest grows arms, squeezing me from the inside, painfully compressing my ribs.

I can't let her weaken me. I can't soften for her.

I can't. I can't. *I can't.*

"Okay, beautiful girl." I swallow over the lump in my throat. "Come find me if you need me."

As much as I want to—as much as I've tried with other women—I can't save her.

I can't save any of them. I can only provide guidance to

help lengthen their stay. And right now is one of those moments when leadership is key.

I stalk from the room, going in search of my friends—my sisters—finding Abi, Chloe, and Nina in the living room, each of them sitting on different armchairs.

"Morning," I offer in greeting.

They turn toward me, their eyes questioning. They won't ask how my night of horrors went. Not verbally, anyway. But I see the need for answers in their matching expressions of concern.

"Did you know Lilly is still in bed?" I ask.

Abi lowers her gaze to the floor.

"She didn't want to join us." Chloe slumps into her chair. "She's given up."

"And I don't know what else to do." Nina pushes to her feet and comes to my side, lightly wrapping an arm around my waist to snuggle into me. "Nothing I say seems to sink in."

"We're all wasting our breath." Abi continues to stare at the carpet. "She'll be gone soon. We're better off getting used to—"

"*Stop*." I warn. "Don't talk like that. *Ever*. Do you hear me?"

They all react in their own defensive ways.

Nina nestles closer into me. Chloe weaves her arms around her waist, self-soothing. And Abi scowls, strengthening her resolve to distance herself from the emotional loss.

"We stick together. Always." I stare at Abi until she meets my gaze. "*Always*."

She winces as Nina nods against my shoulder, the

room filling with silence for a few beats before Abi sighs. "Did you hear about Luther's son?"

"Yes. And I think Luther left a few minutes ago to retrieve him, so we need to prepare."

"For what?" Chloe asks.

"Anything." I inch away from Nina so I can look her in the eye. "We all have to expect the unexpected. Sometimes visitors come and go without drama. But other times…" I let the sentence hang. They've already lived through enough torment to come to their own conclusions.

"What should we do?"

"Start tidying up. Make sure the house is clean. At least that way Luther won't have an excuse for additional punishment." It will also give my sisters something to occupy their minds.

"Fine." Abi huffs. "I'll vacuum."

"I'll dust." Chloe pushes from the sofa.

Nina's tired eyes turn my way. "I guess I'll clean the bathrooms."

"And once I get ready, I'll tidy the kitchen." I attempt to smile and hope I'm exuding calm instead of the nauseating anticipation twisting my stomach. "Don't worry. We'll be okay."

They don't respond to the placation as they leave the room. We all know a threat looms close. It's only a matter of the severity.

I try to follow my own strategy to keep myself occupied as the sand in my mental hourglass dwindles.

I grab a pair of shoes. I do my hair, finger-combing the long strands into a messy plait. The make-up I put on is understated and simple. I don't want to accentuate my features any more than necessary. Only enough for Luther to think I've made an effort.

I'm in the kitchen, wiping down the counter when the faintest sound of an approaching car brushes my ears.

"They're here," Tobias calls from another room. *"My brother is here."*

I stalk into the living room, finding Abi, Nina, and Chloe frantically scrambling to pack their cleaning supplies.

"Don't panic." I maneuver around the coffee table, then the sofa, and squeeze by Nina to get to the curtains and gently glide them an inch aside. "Take a few minutes to breathe."

I listen to my own advice and slow my inhales, expelling the air from my lungs gradually as Luther and Chris stride toward the house. But it's the men climbing from the parked car who steal my attention.

They're both tall, broad, with one man looking toward the house to reveal a face resembling Luther so closely it's clear he must be the son.

My hatred is instantaneous.

No introduction is necessary to determine he's the scum of the earth. Not when I've already heard enough whispers to know this confident man lazily strolling for the mansion doors is yet another monster.

"Go get Lilly." I glance over my shoulder and meet Nina's gaze. "Reassure her everything will be fine."

She nods and quickly leaves the room, Abi and Chloe following behind her while I release the curtain to fall back into place.

The front door opens in the distance. Tobias greets them with words I can't decipher before he rushes back down the hall in the opposite direction. Heavy footsteps approach, accompanied by murmurs from men without souls.

I toe off my shoes and creep across the room, listening, eavesdropping, and plaster myself to the wall beside the doorway. I hear disjointed conversation as they approach, none of which makes any sense. Then I spy a glimpse of Luther and Chris as they pass the living room and continue toward the back of the house.

Their guests walk by a few seconds later, and I stiffen at the malevolence ebbing from them. I can feel their malicious intent.

I wait for the footsteps to move farther along the hall before I attempt a peek around the doorway. The Luther lookalike is focused, eyes straight ahead, while his companion carries his menacing frame with confidence. He's strong, his suit-covered frame hiding what I assume is a lethal body beneath.

I need to see his face, though. To stare into those soulless eyes and determine what I'm up against. But it's too risky now. I won't bring unnecessary attention to myself by greeting these assholes before I'm summoned.

Below the radar is where I fly.

I silently inch back into the living room, prepared to remain in hiding until I can make an escape to find my sisters, when the face-less man glances over his shoulder.

I pause.

Freeze.

I hold my breath as his face comes into view. The deep scowl. The tight-pressed lips. The aura of a brutal man filled with darkness. And as his intense eyes narrow precisely on mine, his harsh attention fills me with dread.

2

PENNY

I HOLD HIS GAZE AS HIS BROWS PULL DEEPER, THE SLIGHT
flare of his nostrils increasing my fear.

He's angered at the sight of me. Furious.

I fight all the instincts screaming at me to run and
begin to breathe again when he turns away, continuing
around the corner, the door to the outside entertaining
area closing moments later.

"Oh, God." I collapse against the wall, sucking in gulps
of air.

Each blink brings back a memory of hard eyes and an
even harder scowl. Like every other man to walk through
the front doors, Cole's companion didn't have an ounce of
pity for my situation.

There was no surprise. No concern.

But there wasn't a taunting smirk either. His expression
didn't hold the conniving prelude I've witnessed from the
vilest of Luther's guests.

The patter of small feet rushes down the hall, forcing
me to put my game face on right before Tobias runs into

the room and skitters to a stop before me. His eyes are big as saucers, his inhales rampant.

"He's here… my brother." He waves a hand for me to hurry. "You need to come meet him."

"I'll be there in a minute."

"No." He shakes his head as Abi, Nina, and Chloe come to stand in the doorway behind him. "Dad wants to see you *now*."

"Toby, I said I'll be there in a minute. I just need to do something first." I have to claim a moment to gain my composure. I can't face a pack of wolves unless I'm in control.

He frowns, his annoyance beyond clear. "But Penny—"

"I need to put on my shoes. Is that okay?"

His stern expression remains in place, yet those innocent eyes lose their anger. He's torn. Nothing is more important than pleasing his father, but he hates upsetting me, too.

"Hurry." He turns on his heel to walk between Abi and Nina. "Don't take too long."

"I won't."

My sisters look at me, their expressions questioning.

"Play it safe," I whisper. "Nod and agree with everything they say. Don't retaliate to anything. Don't smile. Don't talk unless spoken to."

Abi and Nina nod.

"Did you see him?" Chloe asks. "What does he look like?"

"It doesn't matter. Be smart and you'll be okay."

"Hurry up," Tobias calls from down the hall.

I sigh. "You heard the little Nazi. Go. Get the introduction over and done with. I'll be out there soon."

They follow my instruction, leaving me alone to suck in deep lungfuls of air, the oxygen taking long moments to settle me into some semblance of control.

I tiptoe into the hall, clinging to my shoes as I measure a calm stride past the rooms with an armed guard. I run once I'm out of sight until I reach the other side of the house, closing in on the window closest to the outdoor dining setting.

The male voices are almost decipherable from here, the chitchat easily heard over the soft whir of the mist fan.

I want to know what they're here for. If their taste in perversion is more sinister than we're used to I need to prepare myself and everyone else, too.

I inch aside the curtain, chancing another peek.

Luther, Cole, and the man with the harsh stare all sit on the expensive furniture. I can't clearly see their faces, only the back of Luther's head and two stony profiles. But the heir to this lawless empire is still unmistakable.

Cole sits with the same confidence as his father—his shoulders strong, the tilt of his chin arrogantly high. The other man is more laid-back, his demeanor now entirely casual as he talks to Luther about the necessity for regular servicing of sex slaves.

His words chill my veins.

I was right. This man is heartless. Soulless.

"What the fuck do you think you're doing?" Chris growls.

I drop the curtain and swing around to face him entering the dining room. "I was checking to see how many guests we have." I straighten to my full height and pretend I'm not one wrong answer away from punishment. "I assume Luther wants me to organize refreshments."

He eyes me with predatory intent as his lips kick into a smirk. "You're right. He does." He strolls forward, skirting the dining table, not stopping until he's a foot away. "But that doesn't mean you weren't snooping." He reaches out, slowly gliding a hand around my waist, then farther to grab the flesh of my ass.

I tense, every muscle pulled taut through the degradation.

He won't hurt me, though. He wouldn't dare.

As far as he's concerned, I'm off-limits. Nobody gets to defile Luther's precious Penny. But that doesn't mean he can't play games and get me in trouble.

"What would Luther think if he found out you were spying?" he murmurs. "What do you think he would do to you?"

"I wasn't spying. I only wanted to know how many guests there are."

He inches closer, toe to toe, hip to hip, and grinds the hard length of his cock into me. "Are you sure?" He leans in, his mouth a breath away from my cheek. "I don't think I believe you, and I wouldn't be a valued employee if I didn't tell Luther what I caught you doing."

Anger heats my chest, his power sickening me. "Tell him whatever you like. Your threats mean nothing to me."

"Sure they do," he purrs. "Don't pretend you're not scared."

His toxicity invades me, curdling my emotions. I want to lash out. To tell him he's nothing but a leashed dog who jumps at his owner's command. Instead, I pull back and look him in the eye. "I was determining how many guests we have. And now that I'm aware, it's time for me to prepare refreshments."

He chuckles, the tone sinister. "Come on, pretty Penny. Admit your little heart is pounding at the thought of me fucking you."

"Luther would cut off your hands."

"You're right." He drops his hold and steps back with a non-committal shrug. "I guess I'm left to take out my frustration on poor Lilly. You realize she's still all alone in your room, right?"

Defeat hits me.

It's a hard punch to the stomach I can't take without lowering my head to hide my suffering.

I don't see Chris grin in response. I don't need to. I already know his mouth is spread wide, his eyes glistening with victory. His reaction is as predictable as the change in seasons.

I inch away, sliding between him and the dining table, then stalk from the room and into the kitchen. I ignore my turmoil as I put on my shoes, then pull a bottle of scotch from a cupboard. I suppress all the unwanted feelings threatening to overwhelm me while I grab liquor glasses and a serving tray.

What I can't do is pretend Chris won't make good on his promise.

He always does.

The only thing I can do is live with the guilt that I taunted him into taking his frustration out on my sister.

I grind my teeth and tighten my grip around the neck of the scotch bottle until my fingers ache in protest. I'm still there, strangling the liquor when the sound of the sliding door opens down the hall and the clap of numerous sets of heels approach.

Nina, Abi, and Chloe make their way into the kitchen, Tobias following them with tight-knit brows.

"Dad is looking for you," he snips. "He's gone to the bathroom, but he's not happy you've made them wait."

"I'm on my way." I pour a finger of scotch into each glass. "Abi, can you check on Lilly for me?" I give the woman a pointed look, then do the same with Chloe and Nina. "Chris was headed to our room and I want to make sure the two of them don't have another fight."

Abi's eyes narrow in understanding. "Sure." She nods and stalks from the kitchen, Chloe and Nina following.

I ignore Tobias as he continues to scowl in my periphery and grab the tray, my heart pounding beneath tightening ribs as I stalk for the hall leading to the sliding door. The glass is open an inch, letting me hear the soft murmur of Cole and his accomplice.

I can't make out the conversation, only the hushed tone.

There's nothing sinister in the voices. If anything, it's more tinged with conspiracy. Secretive and low.

I suck in a deep breath and square my shoulders as I use the toe of my shoe to slide the door wide. The tap of my heels is almost deafening against the tile. The beat of my heart is even louder.

The men stop talking on my approach, the descending silence thick and uncomfortable. Maybe I should've waited for Luther to finish in the bathroom. If these strangers don't know the rules—if they're unaware I'm not to be touched—I could be standing before a viper pit.

But it's too late to back out now.

I won't scamper away and trigger any sort of predatory chase.

Luther's son meets my gaze, his dark eyes scrutinizing. I quickly lower my focus, not wanting unnecessary attention as I place the tray on the coffee table and grasp two glasses of scotch. I hand the first to his associate, keeping my attention lowered to forgo another scorn-filled look.

I'm surprised when he grasps the offer gently, his large fingers smoothly wrapping around the rim of the glass. That doesn't mean I don't picture the same grip wrapping around a woman's neck, the effortless glide becoming tight. Squeezing. Choking.

How many times has he tortured the defenseless?

I back away and hold the second glass out to Cole. Just like the other man, his intent toward my offering is slow and calm. There's no rough grab or harsh snatch. He reaches out, preparing to take the scotch, then doesn't grasp the glass. His hand only hovers close without contact.

"Aren't you going to introduce yourself?" His tone holds the same arrogant authority as his father. The same superior self-worth I've come to despise.

I swallow over my hatred and chant a mental warning to remain civil.

"I'm Cole," he continues. "Luther's son."

I'm sure he knows I'm well aware of who he is and what he's capable of. This friendly introduction is merely a taunt.

I raise my gaze, answering him with a spiteful look. It's impossible to play nice, especially when I've conditioned myself to be vicious to all men.

"Have we met?" He rakes his gaze over me, from head to toe and back again. "I'm sure I've seen you before."

I don't know what he's angling for—familiarity? Kindness? Or worse, my vulnerability?

"You're mistaken." I shove the glass into his hand and backtrack. I'm ready to turn on my heel and flee inside when the glass door slides open and Luther ruins my chance of escape.

"Ahh, there she is." He strides toward me, sickening pride ebbing off him in waves before he wraps his arm around my waist, awakening my bruises as he drags me into his side. I flow with the movement, not giving him an opportunity to scold me.

"I see you've already met my pretty Penny." Luther tangles his fingers in my dress, reminding me my body is his to control. "I shouldn't have favorites, but it's no secret this woman has claimed all my attention."

"I can see why." Cole continues to eye me, the visual sweep a violation all on its own. "Is there a reason why I feel like we've already met?"

Luther pauses for a moment, glancing between me and his son. "I don't know. Maybe you've seen her on the television. Penny's not from Oregon. But the news of her disappearance may have crossed state lines."

"Penny?" the companion asks. "That's her name?"

Despite knowing I'm not to be touched by anyone but Luther, my unease is high over my status as the center of attention. My position is precarious. Even though these men might not have their way with me, it doesn't mean Luther can't demand I put on a deplorable performance.

It wouldn't be a first.

"Is something wrong?" Luther eyes Cole and grabs the

remaining glass of scotch from the tray before taking a seat. "Have you two met before?"

"No." Cole's interest evaporates. "She must have a familiar face. That's all."

"I'm not sure about her face, but she has a truly unforgettable mouth." Luther laughs. "Don't you, baby girl?"

Humiliation burns holes in my chest as I smile and silently wish I had the power to slaughter them all. I picture myself grabbing Luther's glass, smashing it against the coffee table, and stabbing the jagged remains into his neck.

I could do it, too.

I could kill him. I *would* kill him. If only I wasn't scared of whatever new hell I'd be flung into when someone else claimed me as their possession.

I take a backward step, distancing myself from temptation.

"Where are you going?" He pats his lap. "Come here."

My stomach twists.

I need to check on Lilly. I need these men to find another focus.

But I also need to remember I have no choice.

I reluctantly sulk forward, taking note of the strangers who track my movements.

"Come on." Luther lashes out, grabbing my wrist to yank me down to him. "There's no need to be shy."

I stumble into his lap, my back ramrod as his calloused palm lands on my thigh to hold me in place. It's a familiar scene—my ass against his crotch, his hand a tormenting reminder against my skin, his audience held captive.

He drags the material of my dress higher and higher with the slide of his palm toward the apex of my thighs.

My skin shudders with an outbreak of goosebumps as I brace myself for violation. Soon I'll have to fight. To scream and kick and thrash because that's all part of the performance.

As the seconds tick by to my opening act, I focus along the oceanic horizon. I try to make the picturesque scenery soothe me. But the hard stare of Cole's companion from my periphery is a threat I can't ignore.

He's glowering at me, his nostrils flaring.

He wants me. I can see it in his eyes—the determination. The severity.

He barely blinks as he holds my gaze, not lowering his attention to the thigh Luther continues to expose.

Perhaps it's because his lust is threadbare. Is he dying for a taste or a touch?

"I don't mean to cock block," he drawls, "but is that food still on the way?"

I stiffen, confused.

"I'm starving." He turns his attention to Cole. "And you haven't even eaten today."

Luther's hand pauses on my thigh. The filthy sense of approaching doom dissipates. I'm just not sure if I'm receiving a reprieve or merely being toyed with.

"Yes. Food." Luther slaps my leg, the sting rushing through me as he shoves me from his lap. "We need to feed our guests."

I stagger to my feet, baffled. The gift of my degradation has never been rejected before. My humiliation has always been a coveted prize.

I'm so completely caught off guard I have to force myself to snap out of the bewilderment and hustle to the door to slip inside.

But I don't leave. I remain close to the glass, my heart in my throat as I listen to the disjointed conversation filtering through the barrier.

Their words are hard to hear over the rush of blood in my ears. There are references to a personal harem and I'm sure it's Cole's associate who announces he'd "part ways with a lot of money for just a taste."

So why did he reject the full dose of my humiliation?

I nudge the door wider, hoping for clearer insight, only to panic at the soft footfalls approaching from behind me. I swing around, praying I don't get caught snooping for a third time when Abigail creeps into the hall.

"What are you doing?" she whispers.

I wither in relief and place a hand to my chest, hoping to soothe my ragged heartbeats. "Nothing. Where's Lilly?"

"Chris got to her before we did."

"And?" My turmoil returns faster than it receded.

She cringes. "He messed around with her a little but got frustrated with her tears. She doesn't fight back anymore. She just lays there, playing dead. Now she won't stop sobbing. What should we do?"

We should make him pay. Humiliate and violate. I could spend days—weeks—torturing him before I stole his final breath. But wishes are for those with luck and we have none.

"Get her out of bed. Make her shower. Then force her to eat. Keep her busy the best you can," I explain. "If we occupy her mind we might be able to buy her more time."

She nods and focuses outside. "Are you going to tell me what they're talking about out there?"

"I don't think we need to worry about Luther's son." I

reach behind me and close the door. "Their focus seems to be food, not play."

For the moment, at least.

"Are you sure?"

"For now." I walk by her, heading for the kitchen. "I need to prepare them something to eat. Take care of Lilly until I can get to her."

I don't look back. I'm too busy rebuilding my walls. Creating strength. Locking down emotion. I need to focus to make sure I'm ready for the imminent threats.

Abi sighs. "But—"

"Go," I grate. "Hurry up."

I stalk into the kitchen and pull open the fridge, struggling to juggle all the roles expected of me. I'm the savior and the victim. The leader and the servant. The nurturer and also so badly in need of nurturing.

And above all else, I'm a mess. Just like everyone else.

I grab an assortment of cheeses, along with grapes and pâté, placing them all on the counter when the sound of the sliding door brushes my ears again.

I keep my focus on the food in front of me, taking my time to place them on a serving platter as I wait for Luther to hurl abuse at me for being an unaccommodating host.

"Penny…"

I freeze at the unexpected voice, the tone far younger than Luther's.

I don't turn. I already know the low, husky cadence comes from the man with the stubbled jaw. The one who stopped the progression of a monster's hand along my thigh.

"My name is Luca," he murmurs. "I work for Cole."

The hairs on the back of my neck prickle. My limbs

tingle with the need to protect myself. His tone may be laced with kindness, but I hear it for the deception it is.

"I know who you are," he whispers. "I know where you're from."

I stiffen as unwanted memories assail me, hitting like a slap across the face. I fight not to remember the long-forgotten place he speaks of—my childhood home. The friendly neighborhood I grew up in. The warmth. The love.

I place both hands on the counter, desperate for the smooth stability, and raise my attention to his. Up close I can make out the harsh hazel irises. They scrutinize me, trying to read my anxious thoughts.

"I know about your family." He flicks a cautionary glance toward the entryway on the opposite side of the kitchen, then returns his gaze to mine as he steps forward. "I can help yo—"

"I think you're confused." I force a smile. "Luther won't share me. So, whatever you're playing at, whatever stunt you're trying to pull, it won't work. I'm not to be touched."

His jaw tightens.

I've spoiled his plan. Or at least I've hit a sore spot. God only knows if this man is smart enough to listen to my caution.

He takes another step. "I don't want to touch you. That's not why I came in here."

"Then stay where you are." I back away. "Don't move another inch."

He doesn't listen. In fact, he grows taller in the diminishing space between us, his presence taking up more room as he creeps closer. "Penny…"

My name on his lips is sickening, the tone placating and authoritative at the same time. "I'm here to help you," he continues. "I can—"

"Stop," I growl. "Whatever you have planned, you'll get caught, then Luther will punish you. It doesn't matter who you think you are. You can't silence me. I'll scream."

His lips press tight. His nostrils flare. Pure frustration ebbs from him yet it's not enough. I need his defeat. I have to know he won't divert his sickening intent toward my sisters.

"I'll let you in on a secret," I whisper. "Luther may act like he's willing to share his harem, but believe me, he's far from generous. As soon as you lay a hand on any of us you'll be indebted to him and he always reclaims what he's owed."

"Luther doesn't scare me." His face softens. "And like I said, I have no desire to touch you."

I glare despite the likely retaliation I'll receive for my insolence. "So, you're one of those role-playing types?"

Each monster has a different strategy. A well-greased kink.

Some enjoy boasting their horrors. And others, like this man, prefer to play nice, luring victims with honey to later strike with sickening poison.

"Don't worry," I add. "Luther enjoys the same type of games. Sometimes he pretends he's had a hard day and wants someone to cuddle up against. But gentle cuddles always turn into vicious hands around a delicate throat. Or gouge marks along tender skin. He likes lulling victims into a false sense of security. I gather that's what you're doing now, right?"

His jaw ticks. "No."

"No?" I quirk a brow.

He holds my gaze, those hazel eyes softening back to their deceptive look of concern. "I want to help you."

"Help keep me in a sexual violation routine? Isn't that what you were discussing earlier?"

"Fuck," he mutters under his breath.

"Yeah," I drawl, despite the pulse building in my throat. This man is getting to me. The initial damage he caused by mentioning my home is eating away at my defenses to leave me vulnerable. "I heard. So stop wasting both our time. I need to get this food outside."

It's a mistake to admit how far I intruded upon Luther's privacy. The truth could come back to bite me. Hard. But the longer this man stares at me, his questionable intent putting me on edge, the more unsettled I become.

I want to believe the feigned sincerity in those eyes. I'd give anything to fall headfirst into his offer for help. If only it wasn't a sickening game.

"You need to trust me." He makes another cautionary glance toward both doorways, then approaches another step.

He's so close the gentle scent of his woodsy cologne burns a trail down my throat to scorch my lungs.

He leans in, his gaze never leaving mine as he murmurs, "I know your brother."

My heart stops, the harsh stab of déjà vu assailing me.

With effortless precision he attacks. Without physical connection. With barely audible words.

I have two brothers. Both of them the most caring, brilliant men in the world, and having this asshole use either one of them against me is despicable.

"Stop it." I keep backtracking, needing to maintain the distance between us. I can't let him push me into my past. I can't fall into that trap. "Leave me alone."

I stalk to the far cupboards and retrieve a packet of wafers. If I don't get outside with food Luther will punish me, and despite his heavy hand being less painful than the thoughts of my family, I won't open myself up to any more torture than I've already received in the last twenty-four hours.

"Listen to me." Luca's heavy footsteps approach, his presence closing in at my back, his hands clasping the counter on either side of my waist.

He traps me.

Cages me.

"I know you, Penny. I know how long you've been missing and that your brother never stopped looking for you until he thought he had evidence of your death."

His words whisper into my ears. The message is pure torture.

There are so many aspects to fixate on. Too many facets to assail me.

My brother stopped looking? *Which* brother? What evidence? Was it the tooth Luther extracted from my mouth without sedation? Or the fist-fulls of hair that have been ripped from my head over the unending months?

No.

It's all lies. All make-believe.

I don't have siblings. I don't have a past.

I suck in breath after breath, trying to ignore how he keeps goading me into a game I'm not equipped to handle. He's deliberately pushing my buttons. This man is merely violating me with mental manipulation instead of physical.

Fuck him.

Fuck. Him.

I swing around to face my tormentor, his body so close, those eyes holding mine. I glare, and glare, and glare some more, but all he does is stare right back. There's still no smirk. He's devoid of the toxicity that usually forewarns of an impending strike.

All he gives me is stony silence while he traps me in the cage of his arms.

"You've got the wrong woman." I raise my chin, strengthening my resolve. "I don't know who you're talking about, but it's not me."

I rebuild my mental walls, frantically attempting to make them stronger and stronger as he remains a brutal force in front of me.

I have no family.

No weaknesses.

No vulnerabilities.

There's only here and now. There's only Luther and this unending hell.

"I know you're scared." He gentles his voice, the delicate sweep of his breath brushing my lips. "But I know who you are. There's no mistaking it."

His softness is foreign. The look in his eyes is, too. Everything about him screams of sanctuary, but it's all a trick. A twisted, manipulative strategy.

"Stop it." I glance away. Each inhale is pained, the air filling my lungs carrying tiny thorns to pluck me from the inside out. "Leave me alone."

He's triggering my hope and there's nothing more

dangerous to my stability. My hands shake from the internal battle of optimism and reality. I have to harden myself, to remember all the things I've endured and how the living nightmare never ends. There's no savior. No peace to come.

There're only beatings. And rape. And eventually, the peace of death.

"He lives in Portland," he continues to stoke my insanity, making my pulse spike. "I've been working with him."

"Stop." I squeeze my hands into fists, digging my nails into skin. He's filling my head, suffocating me with lies. I don't want to drown. Not from this. Not from longing.

It's too much.

My lungs squeeze.

My heart hurts.

"He's been dating—"

"*Stop*," I scream, my hand lashing out to slap across his cheek. "*Stop*."

My palm burns with the contact, the pain quickly sliding into my chest, restricting my air.

Oh, God.

He snaps ramrod straight, his eyes blinking in a daze.

Oh, God.

I hyperventilate through the mania, not realizing the stupidity of my mistake until the dark red of my attack seeps across the left side of his face.

Oh, God. Oh, God. Oh, God.

The damage I inflicted is blindingly obvious. It's a mark of defiance. Undeniable evidence of my rebellion.

"It's okay." He backs away. "Don't panic."

It's too late for that. I'm in full-blown hysteria, my

breathing rampant as the glass door slides open down the hall and pounding steps approach.

"What's going on?" Luther's bellow echoes off the walls moments before he enters the room, Cole hot on his heels, both their rage clear to see.

Bile rises in my throat. My limbs tremble.

I huddle into the corner of the kitchen, clutching the counter on either side of me as Luca raises his hands in surrender.

He looks guilty, like he's the one who just threw away his life instead of me.

"Someone better start talking," Cole snarls. "My patience is growing fucking thin."

I can't speak. I can't think.

Luther will rain hell down on me for this. He'll take pleasure in the break of my bones.

"He didn't do anything." Tobias's timid voice carries from the doorway on the far side of the kitchen, his head poking around the frame from the hall.

My heart becomes a fragile butterfly, each violent beat threatening to break the thin membrane of my sanity and send me nose-diving.

He heard.

He heard, and he'll do absolutely anything to make his father proud. Even if it means stabbing me in the back.

"You saw what happened?" Luther asks.

"I was snooping." Tobias inches into the kitchen. "I know I shouldn't, but Penny sounded upset and I was worried."

"And?" Cole growls. "What happened?"

"Nothing. The man was being nice and Penny was..."

Tobias glances at me, killing me with his guilt before he hangs his head.

I don't know what's worse: his conflict over betraying me or the inevitable possibilities if he tells the truth.

"What, son?" Luther approaches him, placing his evil hands on the boy's slight shoulders. "What was she doing?"

I silently beg Tobias to keep quiet. To lie. To betray his father even though I know he never will.

"She was being mean."

Pain slices through me, a soundless sob clogging my throat.

Luther grows an inch with his palpable fury. "You dare to make a guest of mine unwelcome?" He turns toward me, approaching with menacing steps.

I cower, turning my face away, wrapping my arms around my middle. I can't help the show of weakness. I'm fucking bathing in it, my fragility clear for everyone to see.

That man—that stranger—has fractured a resolve I'd built over years of torture. And he did it all with a few perfectly chosen words.

"I'm sorry," I plead. "I don't know what came over me."

"Fucking stupidity, that's what." Luther looms above me, fists clenched at his sides. "Do you need to go back to basic training? Or maybe I should send you to work with the majority of my women so you can understand how well you're treated here."

Horror consumes me.

"Please." I collapse onto my knees. "I didn't mean it. I apologize."

"It's my fault." Luca's voice breeches my nightmare. "I

got carried away. I tried to make small talk and when I mentioned her past I think she took it as a taunt."

I hold my breath, the burn of building suffocation sliding through my veins. I don't understand his motive for taking the fall. Why would he? Why risk his safety for mine?

Luther grabs my chin, his rough grip forcing me to meet his gaze, his other hand raised in threat. "You need to be punished for your disobedience."

I know.

God, how I know.

And I'll accept his violations without protest over the hell of being sent away from here. He can hurt me as much as he likes as long as I don't have to step foot inside one of his brothels.

"Dad," Cole warns. "I'm growing tired of the adolescent distractions from these women. Can't we get the fuck out of here already?"

My heart stutters. Stops.

I don't want a delayed sentence. Giving Luther more time to think is dangerous. I need him to react on instinct, not with well-thought-out deviance.

When Luther doesn't respond, Cole huffs.

"Fine. We'll leave." He starts toward the doorway, murmuring something to Tobias along the way before he disappears down the hall.

I don't drag my gaze from my tormentor. I don't quit praying for him to strike. Not even when Luca's intense stare remains potent in my periphery.

I ignore the jagged seed of hope he planted under my skin. I fight to claw myself back to stability as I blink the heat from my eyes.

Maybe if I hadn't been here so long I could fall heavily into the fantasy of Luca being my savior. Back then I would've done anything, *given* anything for a warrior to haul me out of this nightmare.

But I've learned the hard way that there's no escape from this hell. And my reality is only cemented in place when Luca follows after Cole, leaving me alone with a little boy who betrayed me and a vicious man who I know is more disgusted in my show of weakness than my rebellion.

3

PENNY

Luther didn't hit me.

He did far worse. He left me kneeling on the cold tile, my thoughts in turmoil as he stormed from the kitchen.

I don't know where he went. Chloe informed me that Chris drove them from the house. Cole and Luca included. But even with the distance between us, it took hours to steady my rampant pulse.

"What are you going to do?" Lilly snuggles in bed behind me, returning the comfort I gave her earlier in the day, while the other women remain in their beds. "He's going to be horrible to you."

"I'll do what I've always done—be strong and fight back."

I spent the entire day, and well into the night, berating myself for falling victim to something I've built walls against since my first days in this living nightmare. I never should've taken Luca's bait. I'd thought I was immune to those types of taunts.

I'd thought my defenses held more strength.

"Where do you think they went?" Abigail asks from the bunk above. "They've been gone a long time."

"It's an event night." I clutch my pillow close to my chest and try to lessen my self-pity with thoughts of all the women currently being violated to make Luther money. "He won't be home until after midnight."

I still have a few hours.

I tucked Tobias in bed earlier and collapsed onto mine within minutes. Tomorrow will be challenging and I want to be at the top of my game. Not that sleep feels likely to bless me tonight.

"Are you ready to tell us what happened?" Chloe positions herself up on one elbow from the farthest bottom bunk. "What did that man do?"

I sigh.

I should tell them the error of my ways. Make it a learning experience. But the wound is still raw.

I'm humiliated by the few seconds of hope Luca awakened.

And frightened over how susceptible my family made me.

I have to work harder to forget them. I can no longer simply file their memories away in the back of my mind.

I need to eradicate every thought.

There were never any brothers who kept the sleazy teenage boys at bay. The tight-knit family didn't exist. There was no generous, nurturing mother.

It was all a punishing dream.

"We can talk about it in the morning," I murmur. "I'm too tired now."

"Tobias mentioned the man being nice to you." Abigail speaks softly. "Is that true?"

"Tomorrow, Abi."

"But what if he can help us?" Chloe asks. "If he was nice maybe he can—"

"He can't help us." I add steel to my tone. "Nobody can. The sooner you realize that, the easier each day will become."

The room falls silent.

I hate crushing their hopes. But it's a necessary evil. I'm being cruel to be kind.

"I'm sorry," I whisper. "I just don't want any of you to become optimistic. It's better to expect the worst. One day we'll get out of here, but it won't be because some dark prince came to rescue us. We'll be freed because we were smart and strategic. We don't rely on others. Least of all men who are associated with Luther."

They remain quiet, none of them accepting my apology because they're still holding out for a hero.

I lay there in the bitter void for hours, long after Lilly falls asleep snuggled against me and Nina lets out a soft purr of slumber.

Like I anticipated, it's well after midnight when the sound of a vehicle approaches outside.

Two car doors slam and moments later the thunderous footsteps of men ricochet off the walls. Lilly startles awake beside me. Chloe springs upward.

"Relax," I whisper. "They just got home. You can go back to sleep."

I wince through the placation because I'm not entirely certain everything is going to be okay.

Luther and his goons have been gone all day. He's had enough time to stew on my behavior. To scheme.

Those pounding footsteps could be a sign of his

renewed aggression toward me. The forewarning to a brutal punishment.

The bright glow of the hall light flicks on, seeping into our room from the gap around the door.

There's murmured conversation, then Tobias's sweet voice saying, "But Baba, I want to go back to sleep."

"He woke Tobias," Lilly whispers. "Why would he do that?"

A rumble of chatter builds in the hall. A dark, aggressive reaction to the little boy's protest, which encourages my heart to beat faster.

I throw back the covers, crawl to the end of the mattress, then tiptoe my way to the door.

"What are you doing?" Nina peers down from the top bunk. "Get back in bed. If you're caught snooping…"

She doesn't finish her sentence. She doesn't need to. I already know the consequences and I don't quit my approach. I don't stop until my ear is placed to the doorframe and the now softened conversation becomes clear.

"We need to work together, son." It's Luther, his lowered tone filled with discipline. "This is important."

"Okay, Baba," Tobias replies. "But I'm tired."

The booming footsteps return. Approaching.

"Get back in bed," Abigail hisses.

I could.

I should.

But the thunder is too close. If Luther opens the bedroom door, I'll be caught scampering away.

I'd prefer to have him find me standing here—strong and sure—than see my weakness for a second time today.

Then the door is flung open and my heart squeezes.

I stiffen, facing the devil head on, his face partially

shadowed, the light from the hall beaming down behind him.

He doesn't show surprise over my snooping. He doesn't express annoyance or delight either—just a stony mask of determination while Tobias stands like an exhausted angel by his side.

"You're coming with me." Luther lunges forward and grabs my wrist. "Chloe, you need to join us, too."

He doesn't wait for her to comply. He drags me into the hall, making me stumble as I cling tight to my refusal to show fear.

Gasps and whispers erupt from my bedroom as I'm taken from my sisters. I'm tugged toward the front of the house and into the living room with Tobias dragging his feet behind us.

Questions clog my throat. The need for answers is brutal. But I won't voice my weakness. I have to stay strong this time.

Chris stands at the far edge of one of the cream leather sofas, his expression tight, while one of the silent armed guards disappears through the doorway across the other side of the room, apparently satisfied Luther can handle the situation on his own.

It's safe to assume this is the start of my punishment, and the situation is made all the worse when Chloe inches into the room, her long dark hair loose around her shoulders, her skin pale.

Those sad eyes make me fragile. The tremble in her hands and lower lip are another battle I have to win in an effort to remain strong.

But the surprising thing is, both my tormentors aren't in their usual mocking, sadistic mood. Usually, I'm disciplined out of delight.

Tonight is different.

Luther and Chris appear frustrated, their hard eyes and tight features exuding anger.

The hairs on the back of my neck rise in foreboding. My fingers and toes tingle with anticipation of the unknown. This show of animosity can't be due to my outburst today. It can't. I've never seen these men so venomous toward me.

"Sit," Luther barks.

I comply, sinking into the cream leather, my hands in my lap, my fingers playing with the sheer material of my nightgown. Chloe takes her place on my left, her breathing shallow and ragged.

Luther moves to stand before us and indicates for Tobias to sit on the other side of Chloe. "You need to do something for me."

I hold my breath, unsure if he's talking to us as a collective or the boy on his own.

Having Tobias here must be another punishing strategy.

I knew this day would come—the moment when the child I helped raise would be used as a weapon against me. I'd known and still I hadn't been able to distance myself from caring for him.

"You made a mistake today," Luther growls at me. "A big one."

My pulse pounds everywhere. In my throat. My ears. My wrists. No place more painful than my chest.

"I'm sorry." The apology fumbles from my numb lips. "I lost myself. I promise I'll never do it again."

I promise to never, ever let hope blind me.

"I can make this right." I meet his gaze. "You know I can."

"Yes, I do." He inclines his head. "And you can start now."

I wait for him to lower his zipper and demand a vile act. Instead, he surprises me by reaching into his suit jacket to pull out two white tubes.

He hands one to Tobias and the other to me, the warm plastic smooth against my fingers.

"What's this, Baba?" Tobias asks.

I glance down at the instrument in my fingers, the cylindrical device resembling something akin to an EpiPen.

"Be very careful." Luther kneels in front of his son. "What you have in your hands is a device that can put someone to sleep."

Someone? Or me?

My thoughts rage into a tailspin.

I fight and claw not to show panic but I know Luther too well. I'm certain he's concocted an elaborate *Hunger Game*-type scenario where I'm pitted against a child I would never harm and a sister I adore.

Luther turns his focus to me. "Both of you need to do something really important. And there's no room for error."

"You want us to put someone to sleep?" I straighten my shoulders. "Who?"

"My son's associate." He pushes to his feet as I clench my fingers around the device, attempting to stop the shake of my hand. "I assume you'll enjoy the task seeing as though you felt inclined to attack him earlier."

Shock overwhelms me.

Shock and a whole lot of confusion.

"What about me, Baba?" Tobias's voice trembles. "What do I do?"

Luther pats the boy's head. "Your task is your brother."

My stomach bottoms out as Tobias gasps, his jaw slacking.

"Why?" I swallow over the drought taking over my throat. "And how do you expect a woman and a child to overpower two full-grown men?"

"You don't need to overpower them. You only need to get close enough to stab that device."

"But Baba…" Tobias pleas. "I don't want—"

"You're not going to hurt your brother, son. You're only going to put him to sleep so we can bring him here." He crouches in front of the child again and places a hand on his knee. "His friends haven't been very nice to him. They're teaching Cole bad things about us. But once you put him to sleep, we will bring him back here and talk some sense into him."

It's a kidnapping. Of his own adult son. Facilitated by a fucking child.

"And what happens to Luca?" I stare at my tormentor, searching for answers.

He glares. "That's none of your concern. If I were you I'd take this opportunity as a godsend. You're not my most-favored possession at the moment."

Despite the fear coursing through my veins, I return his pointed look. I curl my lip and hope to remind him why I've always been his favorite.

I'm strong.

I'm a fighter.

The tactic works. His eyes soften. His tight lips twitch into a sly grin.

I raise my chin. "I'll do whatever needs to be done."

I know this task won't buy my forgiveness. The only way I can earn back my coveted position in this house is in the bedroom, under his body and beneath his fists. But I may be able to forego a far bigger penalty.

He smirks. "Good."

Tobias leans forward, peering around Chloe to look at me. To *really* look at me. He's scared. Panicked. He needs me to fight for him. To tell Luther this plan is destined to fail. And God, how I want to battle his demons for him even after he ripped my heart out.

But I can't.

Those sweet, innocent eyes tear me apart one slow blink at a time and all I can do is ignore him. I can't be his champion when my neck is on the chopping block.

I have to stay on the straight and narrow for a while. To obey with complete obedience. To lead my women by example and remind them that additional punishments are only handed out to those who don't play by the rules.

Even though it kills me, I can't win this battle for Tobias.

"What about me?" Chloe remains stock still at my side. "What will I do?"

Luther's lips incline lightly. Chris's do, too.

A skitter of foreboding descends along my spine, the discomfort prickling my skin.

"You, sweet Chloe," Luther purrs, "will be our guinea pig."

4

———

PENNY

The gentle kiss of sea spray brushes my cheeks as the boat bounds across the water's surface.

I hold Tobias at my side, helping him remain upright as we speed through the darkness before sunrise, our vessel quickly approaching an island in the distance.

I'm calm.

Focused.

I've been through a lot worse than stabbing a man with a sedative-filled syringe. And if I succeed, I'm sure I'll live through much more.

I listened with intent as Luther instructed Tobias on how to use the device. He'd told the boy how to hide the cylinder in his long shirtsleeve until the time was right. Then how to jam the tube against a body part, clothing-covered or not, and plunge the leaver with force.

I then watched as Tobias practiced on Chloe as she sobbed and begged him to stop.

Nobody acknowledged her pleas.

Not even me.

All I could do was hold her hand as Tobias jabbed the device against her thigh, then glanced at his father for praise.

I'd been shocked at the drug's quick effect. Panicked, too. The sudden crumple of Chloe's body made me question if something far more sinister had been injected into her system.

Something lethal.

But her pulse remained strong. Her breathing even.

Now, all I have to do is mimic the process, only on a man far bigger and stronger than I am.

There's no room for reluctance. I need to snatch the tube strategically placed in the waistband of my cream pants and strike without hesitation.

That is, if I can get close enough to my target.

"Penny?" Tobias glances up at me, his arms clinging around my hips. His hold tightens whenever we hit a bump in the water, yet the emotion peering up at me has nothing to do with the rough ride.

He's petrified.

Underneath the force calm, I am, too.

The new scenery should be a welcomed distraction from my regular confinement but I don't like being out here. Exposure coats my skin. I lose hold of even more of my strength in this great unknown.

As sickening as it is to admit to myself, I feel more at ease in my gilded cage. I know what to expect in my torture chamber. I'm entirely susceptible here.

"You've got nothing to worry about. You're going to be fine." I fake a smile even though it sickens me to lie to him. "It's all for the best, remember? Your dad is helping Cole. He's taking him away from the bad people."

Tobias's lips move in an indecipherable response. I can't hear him over the rush of ocean and the whirl of wind through my hair.

"It's okay." I crouch to his level and look him in the eye as Luther and Chris stand at the steering wheel a few yards away.

"No. That man was nice to you."

"That man?" I frown. "Your brother?"

"No, the other man. The one you were angry with. He's nice. He's Cole's friend. He's not bad… is he?"

Everything inside me clenches—stomach, throat, lungs.

There's still so much goodness left in this vulnerable child. I'm proud of him for being able to see past his father's lies to think for himself.

"He's not a nice man, Toby." I grab his hand and entwine our fingers. "He only acts that way."

I've had to remind myself of the same truth since the moment Luca approached me in the kitchen.

His intentions weren't kind. They were cruel. He knew exactly what to say to gain a reaction out of me. He's a skilled manipulator. An accomplished sadist.

"Everything will be fine." I squeeze those tiny fingers. "Your dad would never let anything happen to you."

His eyes remain riveted on mine, uncertainty staring back at me.

"I promise." My assurance is yet another lie.

I can't be sure of anything anymore. I'm not even certain this excursion isn't a trick. Or a test. All I know is that Luther will hand me over to his son as a peace offering and then try to facilitate a private moment for me to be alone with Luca.

"Tobias, you're going to make your father proud. He

believes in you and so do I." I stand and turn my attention to the inky ocean, no longer able to watch his suffering. "We'll be okay."

We continue to bound over the water's surface, the tiniest glow of the upcoming sunrise barely visible against the boat's bright headlight.

A darkened pier comes into view on the island we approach, with another boat lying in wait. Slowly, a man is illuminated, his features unmistakable even from this distance.

Cole.

He's wearing a business suit, his tight expression a clear indicator of our lack of welcome.

His demeanor doesn't change when the boat's engine is cut and the vessel is tied in place alongside the pier. He just stands there, tension ebbing off him.

"What are you doing here?" He crosses his arms over his chest, his stylish jacket defining his muscled arms and shoulders.

"Morning, son." Luther walks to the side of the boat and holds out his hand for me to take. "We need to talk."

I remain quiet as I'm helped from the vessel, my bare feet dragging along the wooden pier.

I let their conversation wash through me. I acknowledge the aggressive chitchat and Luther's promise of not being armed. But my attention is focused on the darkness of the island, trying to find the target for my attack.

Luca isn't in sight.

He's not here to protect his boss. He's not the one patting down Luther or Chris—that task is left to Cole.

It isn't until the cold eyes of his son hit me that apprehension truly takes hold.

He's so much bigger than I am. And from memory, Luca was even larger in frame. Those meaty fists could knock me unconscious in seconds. Those hands could snap my neck in an instant.

"If you came to talk," Cole mutters, "why did you bring a woman and child as a shield?"

"A shield." Luther balks. "Do I need one against my own son? Because I brought her here as a peace offering. The woman is yours."

I'm shoved toward Cole, my footsteps fumbling.

"You're handing her over?" He scrutinizes me.

The weight of his appraisal is heavy. Cloying. The pinpoint focus makes me itch to brush my fingers over the hidden plastic tube to make sure it's not going to fall from my waistband.

I drag my gaze away to stop the nervousness from taking hold. I return my focus to the island. I work harder to find a man hiding in the scrub as Luther attempts to manipulate his son into inviting us up to the house, using Tobias's fatigue as an excuse.

They continue to argue under a tone of barely contained civility until finally Cole complies with a, "Fine. Go ahead."

He indicates for me to start walking. For *me* to lead us into battle.

I don't move.

Unease hits me like a freight train.

"Penny." Luther waves a hand, instructing me to hurry. "You first, my sweet."

My pulse catches at the endearment. *No*, it's a blatant warning.

I have no choice but to obey. I have to do this to regain my position of menial power. To reassert my strength.

Fuck.

I hold out a hand for Tobias, who walks forward to join me, then we both lead the way to the end of the pier and onto the island.

Murmured words carry from behind us, the subtle timbre letting me know everything remains faux civil as I make my way toward the light of the house up ahead.

Tobias keeps glancing over his shoulder, watching, waiting. I clutch his hand tighter, attempting to calm the tremble of his fingers. It's the only comfort I can provide. There's nothing else.

I can't gush soothing words. I'm unable to lie to him anymore. I can only attempt to give reassurance in the tightness of my hold as we continue along a winding gravel path, bringing us closer and closer to the large expanse of a mansion up ahead.

I take us into a house yard, my feet hitting cool cement tile placed around an immaculate pool.

"I'm scared," Tobias whispers. "I want to go home."

Me too.

"Be strong." I squeeze his sweaty palm tighter. "This will all be over soon."

I reach the glass door leading to the brightly lit living area and stop to wait for instruction.

"Go." Luther comes up behind me, shooing me forward. "Get inside."

"Wait," Cole barks. "You, the woman, and the kid can go inside, but your dog isn't welcome."

The demand twists my stomach.

I look at Chris—*the dog. Disdain crosses his* features as I wait for Luther to voice a reprimand that never comes.

I've never seen anyone disrespect this monster and get away with it. Not once. Not ever.

"Whatever you say," Luther complies.

It's an act. One I can't mimic.

"I guess I'll stay here then." Chris steps away. "Just so you can feel like more of a man for keeping me outside."

Cole claps him on the shoulder as he approaches the house. "If I were you, I wouldn't forget your best buddy ate lead yesterday because of me."

I suck in a breath as white noise assaults me.

Everything stops.

Every. Single. Thing.

Thoughts. Breath. Time.

I glance between the two men as they exchange muttered retorts my mind can't decipher. I'm stunned. Confused. And painfully hopeful.

Your best buddy ate lead.

Should I allow myself the luxury of believing the comment was made about Robert? That the vile, piece of shit might actually be hurt? Or better yet, dead?

He didn't return home with Chris and Luther.

They haven't made mention of him at all.

My stomach heats, the warmth spreading rapidly as Luther stalks toward me, his glare enough of a warning to get me to hustle my ass inside while Chris and Cole continue to swap barbs.

I don't allow hope free rein as I walk into the opulent house. I keep optimism's wings clipped as I take in the open living and kitchen area, the entire space immaculate apart from a few mugs on the dining table.

"Sit," Luther growls. "Here, beside me."

He claims the recliner and pats his hand on the armrest.

I do as instructed, sticking close to my nightmare, not only to be seen as an obedient slave, but to read his energy. I want nothing more than to confirm if the anger simmering below his surface is from the loss of his henchman.

Tobias settles away from us, perching on the opposite sofa, right where Luther foretold him to be—alone, ready for Cole to take a position beside him.

"Where's Luca?" I whisper. "What happens if he's not here?"

"He's here," Luther snarls. "Now quiet."

I snap my mouth shut as Cole enters the house, locking the door behind him and pulling across the sheer curtain. "The boy's no longer glued to your side?" he asks, his attention raking over the boy, then me, to rest on his father.

"We heard you're leaving." Luther shrugs. "I guess he wants to make the most of the moments you have together."

Leaving?

I scramble to understand what must have happened yesterday to cause their sudden departure. They were meant to be talking business. Discussing a partnership.

My outburst couldn't have caused the dissolution of their plans, could it? Surely my mindless rebellion didn't instigate an avalanche. If so, this stab-and-sedate attack won't absolve the mess I've made.

This punishment isn't enough.

Luther will want more from me. He'll want everything.

I clutch my hands in my lap, digging my nails into my palms in an attempt to lessen the instinct screaming at me to fight to the death.

It isn't until my target walks from the hall to take a few steps into the room, his chin high, his intense eyes finding mine, that the noise in my head lessens.

For the briefest second, hope flickers to life.

Painful, delusional hope.

I clench my teeth against the traitorous response as Luca glances away, disregarding me in an instant.

From bliss to devastation in seconds.

Stupidity to reality.

"What's going on?" He flicks his attention to Cole. There's no panic or apprehension. He's entirely mellow. At least on the surface.

"I'm not sure yet. But apparently, my father comes in peace," Cole drawls. "Is my little fox still sleeping?"

"She's back to the same tricks as she was on her first night here."

I sit straighter, trying to hear what isn't being said.

They're talking about a woman. Their own captive.

I hold in a snarl, my previous optimism entirely snuffed by disgust.

I knew I was right not to believe a word Luca said to me yesterday. I *knew* and yet the smallest part of me is still surprised to learn of his depravity.

They continue talking about her while anger coils itself around me, empowering me, making me greedy for my opportunity to strike. This man, with his laid-back air and unconcerned tone, couldn't give a shit about a woman held against her will.

He's just another monster, hiding his true colors behind a handsome face.

"Go check on her," Luther encourages Cole from my side. "By Amar's account, she took quite a beating yesterday. She probably shouldn't be left alone."

They beat her?

My fury increases, my train of thought pinpointing on my upcoming task. I read my opponent as they continue to talk. Luca stands tall, his attention sweeping the room, settling on Cole, Luther, Tobias, and finally me.

Those penetrating eyes narrow. His shoulders tense.

I mimic his posture, sitting a little straighter on the armrest. But I don't narrow my stare. Instead, I soften it.

I preempt Luther's promise to give me an opportunity to get within reach of this slimy devil. I act as if I'm not driven by retaliation. That I've learned my lesson from yesterday's outburst and I'm now a docile puppet who lives to please.

"I'm handing Penny over as a symbol of my apology." Luther's words break my focus. "Why don't you take her to one of the bedrooms and get her accustomed to a new way of life under my son's reign?"

Adrenaline kicks in as Luca glances at his boss with a raised brow. That disgusting tweak to his expression is a clear inquiry for permission. A filthy request to defile me.

"Go." Cole waves him away. "Enjoy yourself."

Luca doesn't move. He remains immobile, his expression still questioning.

"*Go*," Cole barks. "Teach her what she needs to know."

The taste of approaching revenge makes my heart happy despite its panicked beats. I'm going to make this asshole pay for his sins. I'll inject him with this sedative and hand him over to the devil to play with.

Then he can see what it's like to be a victim.

"Remember what will happen if you don't behave." Luther slaps me on the ass and I jolt from the impact. "Now make me proud."

"Of course." I let the words roll off my tongue as I maneuver around the coffee table and into open space to wait for Luca to join me.

He's the one who looks at me with skepticism this time, his hazel eyes wary for brief moments before he leads me into the hall.

The first step away from prying eyes isn't a relief. The solitude with this bulky predator is daunting but I'm determined. Focused. I'll earn my way back into Luther's good graces.

I won't fail.

"Take the last door on the right." He slows his approach, making me take the lead.

There's no excitement in his tone. I'm surprised he's not salivating at the opportunity to violate me. Usually, men get a sly swing in their step when they know their perverted fantasies are about to be fulfilled. They act differently. There's an edge to them.

But not this man. He isn't showing an ounce of enthusiasm.

His bliss is tightly bottled.

As we pass exquisite artwork hung along the walls and the long line of lights in the ceiling, he remains closed off. It isn't until I reach the door and push it wide that he dares to touch me, his arm brushing my shoulder as he reaches inside to flick on the light.

It takes all my restraint not to bristle. Externally, anyway. On the inside I'm coiled tight, my mind primed and ready for me to strike.

"I still don't want to touch you," he snarls. "Just thought you'd prefer to see."

I try to siphon as much information as possible from his actions. I attempt to hear the deceit in his tone, and still I get nothing.

I can't grasp his intent.

I know he has a motive. It's now common knowledge at least one other slave is here. But I continue to struggle with his faux kindness.

"Thank you," I whisper. "The light is appreciated."

I step inside, my spine tingling as I enter a room consumed with his scent. It reminds me of yesterday. Of his kind, lying eyes. Of his conniving deception.

When the door clicks shut behind me there's no stopping my heart climbing into my throat. I can't help thinking about the consequences of a possible failure, not only from Luther, but this brutal man.

His hidden motives taunt me. The walls he's built to hide his true self leave me with no insight of what's to come if I don't succeed.

"What did he do to you?" Luca walks around me, coming to stand like a bulky statue in front of me.

"Excuse me?"

"After we left you behind like fucking cowards," he growls. "What did Luther do to you?"

I bristle, hating his renewed stance on this friendly facade. The building kindness is unsettling. "My punishment is being handed over to Luther's son. And to you."

His eyes narrow, then lower. His attention treks down

my body, scouring every inch of me. And still I don't witness his sexual interest. This man has an uncanny way of hiding his desire.

"You don't seem scared." His gaze slowly returns to mine. "Does that mean you're open to trusting me?"

"Of course." My response slips out too fast, the hint of sarcasm not helping my cause. He needs to think I'm his to break. A toy. A puppet.

He sighs. "I'm not going to hurt you, Penny. You can stay as far away from me as you want, but we need to talk."

No. There's no room for chatter. I don't want him weaving his manipulation into my brain again.

"We're not here to talk." I shuffle closer, bridging the distance between us so there's only a breath of space. I look up at him through my lashes and try my best to appear meek. "You heard Luther. I'm a gift."

I'm not a viper coiled to attack. I'm an object. A slave.

Believe me, Satan.

He stiffens, his jaw twitching a fraction. His eyes narrow, the intensity of his stare making my heart skip a beat.

I wait for him to comply. To finally steal what's right in front of him.

"You're not a fucking gift," he snarls. "You're not a fucking slave. All that is over."

A twinge of yearning plucks at my heartstrings before I quickly shut it down.

"Whatever you say," I keep my voice meek, testing to see if he prefers weak and vulnerable to my usual strong and combative as I avert my gaze like a true submissive. "I'm yours to command. Just tell me what you need."

A growl emanates from his chest, the low rumble inspiring goosebumps along my exposed arms.

"What I need," he grates, "is for you to understand that I don't want to fucking touch you. Not now or in the future. I'm not Luther."

No, he's not.

I'm well aware he's an entirely new monster. One with different intricacies and fetishes.

"I understand." I keep my head lowered, the tube burning hot against my belly. "You're not like other men. You're special."

He scoffs. "No, I'm not. I'm just a guy who wants to fucking help you." He reaches into the back of his jeans and pulls out a cell. "Look."

He presses the screen a few times, then holds it up to me. My heart stops as he scrolls through images, picture upon picture of an innocent girl with a dazzling smile.

"This is you, right?"

It takes long seconds for me to shake my head, denying my past. The woman on the screen isn't me. Not anymore. I look nothing like her. The light left my eyes long ago. The natural exuberance no longer exists. What took its place is the polished beauty paid for by a wealthy sex trafficker. The perfectly waxed skin. The regularly manicured nails and tinted hair. With all these services dished out by people who ignored my plight for freedom.

"I know who you are," he continues. "I know your brother. Decker and I work together. Believe me, I won't do a fucking thing to hurt you. I'm here to help."

Decker.

My surname slices through me with the force of a steal blade.

Neither one of my brothers has ever taken our last name as a nickname. This man is making assumptions. Playing games.

He found my past online and is using the information to continue his trickery.

"You're confused," I whisper. "That's not me. I have no brother."

I focus on letting all emotion slip through me. I don't dwell on the aching memories. I shove everything from my mind, growing hollow... all except for the tiniest flicker of light beginning to creep its way through the darkness of my solitude.

What if he does know one of my brothers? What if he knows the woman I used to be?

I clear my throat, dislodging the instability trying to ooze its way back into me.

I'm not that woman on the screen anymore.

That life belonged to someone else.

There's no family waiting for me.

No love to welcome me home.

"What?" His brows pull tight, his confusion heavy. "Why are you denying it? This is obviously you." He taps the cell screen, scrolling through more triggers, weaving more manipulation.

I can't let him continue.

This has to stop.

"I'm sorry, but you're confused." I step into him and reach for his arm to lower the phone from view. "And besides, who I am doesn't matter when you're here to teach me the ropes."

I grip the softness of his T-shirt and maneuver my

hands beneath the material to place my palms on his stomach. His muscles tense at my touch.

"Penny," he warns. "Stop."

My pulse increases. My chest tightens.

I wait for the usual revulsion to overwhelm me, but the nauseating protest doesn't appear.

For some reason, there's no humiliation. No sickening disgust.

Instead, there's apprehension. Thick and cloying concern.

He's not acting the way I've come to expect from Luther and his men.

He's not devouring this opportunity like a stereotypical predator.

"You don't want me?" I ask, sounding offended. "Aren't I as tempting as your little fox?"

The reminder of the other woman is for my benefit. I need to remember he's not innocent.

"You're a temptation, but not in the way you think." His tone is gentle as he steps back. "You don't need to do this."

He's wrong.

This is exactly what I need to do. I have to get closer. Distract him further. Add more confusion.

"I'm a gift." I grab his belt and begin to pull it from its confinement.

"Jesus Christ. *Stop*." He pushes at my wrists. "Just fucking stop."

He's revolted by me and somehow this humiliation is far worse than what I'm used to.

I'm not good enough for him.

Or maybe I'm too used. Too abused. Too broken.

He has the opportunity to take anything he wants and he hungers for nothing. There's no perversion in his eyes. No deviance.

I don't know what to do. I need to be close. I can't strike from this distance. "Luca, I..."

Words fail me as my cheeks heat in shame.

Has my life sunken so low I now need to beg for violation? Is that where this hellish existence has led to?

"Please," I plea, my humiliation plunging marrow-deep.

"I don't want to fuck you," he snarls. "I want to *help* you."

"Then help me by letting me do my job. Let me make up for hitting you yesterday."

His nostrils flare. "As far as I'm concerned, I deserved your aggression. And I deserve far more for leaving you behind. But for now, you're going to wait in here while I go back out there to keep an eye on Luther."

No. Jesus Christ, *no*.

He can't distract Tobias from his mission. He can't stop me from succeeding, either.

Luca stalks around me, heading toward the door as undiluted fear sweeps through me.

"Wait." I pluck the hidden device from my waistband and tuck it into my palm, keeping the weapon out of view as I scramble to catch up.

He doesn't pause. He gets to the door and reaches for the handle.

This is it. I have to strike.

I run, raising my hand high, then launch myself at him.

5
———

LUCA

HER FRANTIC FOOTSTEPS APPROACH, HER SHADOW QUICKLY climbing across the door in front of me.

I wait until she closes in, her rampant breathing reaching my ears, before I spin around and grab the arm violently charging toward me.

She's got a weapon—some sort of plastic device—but I ignore it for now as I sidestep, forcing her to follow with a jolt of my wrist. She turns with my harsh movements, her lithe body malleable to my direction when I shove her toward the door.

A quick palm against the wood is all that saves her face from sudden impact as I twist her other arm behind her back.

She doesn't cry out. There's no plea for help or scream for salvation.

Instead, her breathing increases, her panic only shown in the short, sharp rasps for air.

"What the fuck?" I snarl in her ear as I focus on the

cylindrical tube she clutches in a white-knuckled grip. "What the hell is this?"

She doesn't respond. There's no struggle or fight, only tightly coiled hostility.

"*What the fuck*?" I repeat, sliding my hold to her fingers to wrench the device from her grip.

"No," she begs. "Don't."

Her plea kills me, fucking strips me bare. I can't believe what I'm doing to such a fragile, vulnerable woman. If only it wasn't clear she was trying to take me down.

"Then start talking." I place my forearm against her back, loosely keeping her trapped as I inspect the weapon. "What is this?"

"Let me go and I'll tell you."

I snicker a scorn-filled laugh, attempting to gain answers through aggressive taunts so I don't have to take alternate measures. "Nice try. But no dice. Tell me what's going on before you get yourself in more trouble."

"Please." Her voice cracks. "You said you want to help me. So help me. Give it back. Let me walk out of here and pretend this never happened."

"No way in hell, shorty."

For starters, I'm not letting her go anywhere near Luther. Not again. Not after I made the mistake of following Cole's instruction to leave her kneeling on the kitchen floor yesterday. And I sure as shit won't be handing over the instrument she felt inclined to stab at my neck.

"Was this your idea or his?" I grip the crook of her arm and turn her to face me, her wide eyes blinking up at me in panic, her skin pale, those ruby lips parted. "Talk," I growl.

"Please don't say anything." Her delicate throat works over a heavy swallow. "It was my idea. Luther doesn't know. He isn't even aware I stole the syringe from him months ago. I just wanted to pay you back for taunting me yesterday."

"Pay me back how? What was the desired outcome? Is this lethal?"

"No." She shakes her head. "It's only a sedative. You would've fallen asleep instead of…" She glances away, her brows pinching.

"Instead of raping you?"

She nods, the movement gentle.

She's such a pretty little liar.

We both know I wasn't about to assault her. I was leaving the fucking room, for Christ's sake.

"Please, can I have it back?" She grates her teeth over her lower lip. "I promise I won't use it."

I hold in a scoff as I remain against her, so close I can hear the gentle rasp of her breath.

She's a contradiction—her body soft yet ready to strike, her dark eyes gentle even though trepidation lingers beneath.

"Please, Luca, it was a mistake." She grasps the top of the device, her fragile hand clasped over mine. "He'll kill me if he finds out. He'll probably kill me when he realizes it's missing from his stash. Let me take it so I can put it back."

I grin, the curve of my lips far from friendly. "But you're a gift, remember? There's no going back."

She should be fully aware there's no returning to Luther unless something else is at play.

"Tell me what's going on." I shove the device in my

back pocket, not allowing her an inch of freedom. "*Now,* Penny."

A ragged exhale shudders from her lips. "You don't understand." She implores me with her frantic tone. "He'll kill me."

"He's not going to touch you."

"Yes, he will. And he'll hurt my friends, too. My sisters. You can't save me."

"Bullshit." I get in her face, eye to eye, almost nose to nose, making sure she's got a front row view to my sincerity. "I *will* save you."

There's no doubt in my mind. She won't leave this island a slave. Not while there's still air in my lungs.

Her gaze hardens, the deep brown turning punishingly dark. "And what about the little fox you've beaten? Will you save her, too?"

She tilts her chin, showing defiance. *Spite.*

She thinks she knows me, thinks she's got me all figured out.

"The beaten little fox isn't a prisoner." I back off, giving her animosity room to breathe. "She's on our side. *Your* side."

"Is that why you beat her?"

"I didn't," I grate. "Robert is responsible for hurting her, but he paid for that mistake with his life."

Her eyes flare.

For a second, the slightest glimmer of hope brightens her features, increasing her beauty, before it's quickly suffocated by suspicion.

"I don't believe you." She shuffles out from between me and the door. "Robert isn't dead."

"I think the bullet that took his life would disagree."

She blinks and blinks, her disbelief lingering. "She killed him?"

"No, Luther did."

"I don't understand." She screws up her nose. "Luther would never—"

"He had no choice. That asshole's death is the only reason Cole is still civil with his father. It's the price he had to pay for what his goon did to Anissa."

"Anissa?"

Fucking hell, I don't have the patience or the time for this. "The little fox," I snap. "Nobody hurts one of ours and gets away with it."

"Oh." Her mouth forms a pouty circle. "I..."

"What?"

She shakes her head. "I don't know... I... I want to trust you. Really, I do." She raises her focus to mine. "I'm just not sure how."

I don't buy it. She's still got tricks up her sleeve and I'm running out of time to figure them out.

"What if I gave you back your weapon?" I hedge. "Would you trust me then?"

Her tongue snakes out to quickly swipe her lower lip. It's devious. "You'd do that?"

I'm fucking tempted that's for sure.

It's those eyes. The strength. She undoes me with her determination despite the shattered pieces of her psyche I itch to place back together.

"Here." I reach into my pocket and pull out the cylindrical tube. "Take it. It's yours."

She inches back, her disbelief a sweet price to pay.

"It's okay." I nudge the device closer to her. "Take it."

Hesitation reclaims her features as she eyes the

weapon, her attention moving from my hand, to my wrist, and farther along my arm.

Fucking subtle.

She's devising another plan to jab me. She practically has *Plan B* written on her forehead in neon.

"Thanks." She steps forward, cautious.

Those delicate fingers brush my skin as she claims her prize.

But the thing is, her touch is worth the upcoming battle. The graze of her fingertips is the softest friction. A hypnotic fucking spell. And when her attention returns to my face I can almost pretend she's peering back at me in sincerity.

Unfortunately, I know better in that regard, too.

She sinks her teeth into her lower lip, trying to play the timid yet thankful role. To get closer. To obtain the perfect vantage point to strike from. It's so fucking obvious it plays out in my head like a movie before she even makes a move.

"Really," she whispers. "Thank you."

I keep my jaw locked and pretend every one of my nerves isn't hyper-sensitive as I tell her, "Don't mention it."

My sincerity doesn't stop her from tightening her grip on the weapon, though. And the resulting twitch of my cock isn't my proudest moment.

Some sick part of me wants her to fight. Adrenaline floods my system at the thought of another reason to grab her.

"How do you plan on getting me out of here?" She creeps closer. "Just because Luther handed me over doesn't mean he'll allow my freedom. It's too big a risk."

"Let me worry about that." I remain still, on alert, patiently waiting.

I should warn her not to follow through with her attack. If I was the good guy I'm pretending to be, I'd tell her to think twice. But she's made it clear she has no desire to give me the truth. Not in words anyway. I'll figure her out from her actions.

"Okay." She nestles closer. "I trust you."

The jut of her hand is quick. Lightning fast. I almost don't catch it in time as she aims for my stomach.

"Too slow." I snatch her wrist before impact, pull her forward, and sweep out my leg to knock her feet out from beneath her. I push her off-balance, delight in her gasp, and keep clinging to her arm as she falls.

I guide her slightly, making sure she doesn't hit the carpet too hard. But then I'm all over her, pinning her body beneath mine and her hands above her head.

"I'm done playing games." I smother her with my weight. "This was never about payback, or getting the syringe to Luther."

She turns rigid, yet again refusing to call for help. It's clear she knows she's on her own. With no one to save her.

Well, she has me now. If only she'd fucking realize it.

"This is the last time I tell you—" I get in her face, her snarled lips a whisper from mine. "—I'm here to fucking save you. You hear me? You're free."

She bares her teeth. Glares. Thrashes.

Again, it's not my proudest fucking moment when my dick enjoys the extravaganza. I don't want to appreciate the way she writhes beneath me. God knows, Decker will kill me if he ever finds out.

"Stop fighting. Stop treating me like the fucking

enemy." I keep her pinned. "That woman you think is here against her will is working with us." I shouldn't be telling her this. It's too dangerous. For her *and* me. "We're taking down Luther's operation. We won't stop until we succeed."

She lessens her fight for freedom.

"It's true," I continue. "The nightmare is over. You're going home. But I need you to tell me if this attack was you. You have to be honest and let me know what I'm up against."

She stares at me, those penetrating eyes scouring my face as if she's searching for the Holy Grail. She's starting to believe me. Finally, I'm getting through to her.

"Do you want me to call your brother? Is that it?" Slowly, I release her hands, keeping my attention on her weapon as I grab the cell from my jeans. "If I get him on the phone so you can speak to him, will you finally quit fighting?"

Her face pales, all the blood draining from her cheeks in an instant. "No." She shakes her head. "I told you, I don't have a brother."

Why the fuck does she keep saying that?

It's crystal clear she's Penny Decker—Sebastian's sister —the woman who was tempted away from the safety of her home by lies Luther fed her about a modelling career. If I've heard the story once, I've heard it a million times.

I know her. I've read the missing persons report. I spent all goddamn night scouring the internet, devouring everything I could find about her.

"Fine." I climb off her, snatching her weapon as I go. "Have it your way." I drop the cylinder to the carpet and crack it beneath my boot.

"*No.*" She scrambles onto all fours and lunges for my feet. "*Don't.*"

"It's done. Gone. Get over it." I press harder, twisting my ankle from side to side as the device fractures. "Now, I'm preparing to go out there, guns blazing, because I've got a feeling this attack wasn't your idea, but I need you to confirm it for me, okay? I need you to tell me, either way, was this you or him? Does Luther have anything else up his sleeve?"

She claws at my boot, thumping and tugging.

"Penny," I snarl. "I need information so I can protect you properly. So I can protect that fucking kid."

She slumps onto her haunches, her face crumpling with defeat.

"You or him?" I repeat.

More than her answer, I want her surrender. I want her to quit fighting and give in to me. To my protection.

"Penny," I warn.

Her head falls back, lulling on her shoulders. I stop breathing as her lips part, her silent acquiescence already the sweetest sound to my ears.

"*Luca.*" Torian's voice punches through my anticipation, his call faint. "*Luc.*"

Panic hits me, but it's the sudden flare of fear in her eyes that makes me freeze. She knows what's going on out there and it's scaring the hell out of her.

"Tell me." I grip her chin. "*Tell me.*"

I should be running for my boss, gun in hand. Instead, I can't drag myself away from her. I tell myself it's only for one more second in the hopes she'll comply. Because information is key, right? I could gain an advantage over whatever the hell is going on out there if only she would give in to me.

"*Luca,*" Torian roars.

Shit.

I shake off my obsession with her and rush for the door, grabbing my pistol from the back of my waistband.

"Luca..."

Her voice is heaven to my ears. If only it wasn't too little too late. I can't hang around any longer.

"Luc, wait."

Fuck.

I turn, finding her staring back at me, her forehead etched in pain.

"He's out to get you." There's remorse in her tone. In her eyes, too. "And I have no doubt he'll succeed."

6

———

PENNY

LUCA DASHES FROM THE ROOM, NOT ACKNOWLEDGING MY pained admission with more than a narrowed stare.

He's going to get himself killed.

All of us could die in the melee.

Oh, God, *Tobias.*

I rush to my feet and scramble to follow him. As I enter the hall, I find Luca crouched before Tobias, a finger to his lips as he instructs Luther's son to remain quiet.

For a brief moment I'm struck with the kindness in his features. The gentle nurturing that seems one hundred percent pure. Then he looks at me, his gaze hardening as he pushes to his feet.

"*Go,*" he mouths to Tobias. "*Hide.*"

The boy rushes toward me and I usher him into the room, mimicking Luca's warning to keep as quiet as possible with a finger to my mouth.

"What's going on?" I whisper.

"Dad told me to come get you. You need to go to him."

I nod. "I will. But first, you have to hide, okay?"

He opens his mouth to protest.

"Not now, Tobias. You need to listen. *Hide.* Get under the bed. Or in the closet. But don't come out, you hear me?"

"What's happening?" His voice breaks with a sob.

"I don't know. I have to go with Luca to find out."

"But you were meant to—"

I shake my head at him, cutting off his words. I'm well aware of what I was meant to do. I know I failed. "Did you do it? Did you sedate Cole?" I murmur.

He winces, his tiny shoulders curling in on themselves.

"Don't worry. You did great." I smile at him, my heart breaking at the thought of this possibly being our final goodbye.

Luther will kill me for failing.

Me, and the man I endangered.

"Now it's important you hide." I shoo him farther into the room and grab the door handle. "Don't come out until I get you."

I want to tell him I love him. There're so many things I need this little boy to know, but I close the barrier between us and force myself to remain strong as I turn to Luca.

He's in the middle of the hall, creeping toward the entry to the living room, his gun raised. He's about to start a war. And with Cole drugged, he'll surely get himself killed.

"Stop," I whisper. I run for him on the tips of my toes.

He doesn't listen, stepping into the light from the main room, his shoulders strong, his face stony as he points his barrel at a target I can't see.

"*Luther,*" he yells. "Drop it."

I skitter to a stop beside him as gunfire rings out, the booming sound pummeling toward us.

Pop.

Pop.

I duck, my pathetic attempt to protect myself improved when Luca shoves me back into the sanctuary of the hall.

I stumble against the wall as he rushes into the living room, more *pop, pop, pops* raining down.

I'm too stunned to scream. I'm completely dazed, and it's not only because of the battle or the shouting voices. It's because Luca shoved me.

Protected me.

In the heat of the moment, when he was surrounded by danger, his first instinct was to push me out of harm's way.

He did as he promised.

He attempted to save me.

I remain immobile as voices brush my ears—the sound of Chris talking from outside, then Luther, and even a slurred response from Cole. Grunts and thumps carry from the main room. There are clear sounds of a struggle and all I can think about is the man who tried to help me. The one who is now eerily silent.

Luther's laugh is the only noise that penetrates my shock, the conniving tone filling me with dread.

"It's too late. I got him," he taunts. "Penny, check to make sure Luca's dead."

Oh, God.

I prop myself against the wall and beg my legs to strengthen beneath me. I can't stop shaking. I can't even breathe properly as I fumble my way to the hall entry and find Luther on the floor, leaning on his elbows, his face awash with smug satisfaction as his son sways on his feet, barely remaining upright.

Their expressions paint a horrid picture—Luther's victorious and egotistical, Cole's devastated and confused.

Guilt has me searching for the man who offered kindness. The one I find shielded behind the back of a sofa, his body lifeless, one cheek covered in blood.

A cry builds in my throat, demanding to be heard. I let the pressure assault me. Punish.

He was my only chance at freedom and I let him slip through my fingers. He was my savior and I treated him like a predator.

"Don't go near him." Cole fumbles over his words. "Get the fuck away."

I ignore him in my need to confirm Luca's death, not only to appease my tormentor, but for my own insight. I have to feel the void where there should be a heartbeat, to let the lack of life slice another scar into my tormented soul.

"Luther, I'm sorry." I inch into the room. "I'm so sorry. I tried to stab him with the sedative but he stopped me. He was too quick." The explanation fumbles from my lips. "I didn't know what to do. I thought maybe I could—"

"Just check him." Luther crawls to his feet.

I do as I'm told, starting toward Luca's prone body, following the crimson trail staining the ivory tiles. I scour every inch of him hoping for movement, my gaze trekking from the heavy boots, along his thighs, across his stomach, to his neck, chin, and mouth. My gaze finally comes to rest on the hazel eyes slowly blinking back at me.

He raises a shaky hand to his lips, requesting my silence.

I should tell Luther. I *need* to inform my owner of the threat, yet the words don't form. I'm incapable of announcing this man's vulnerability. Not after he tried to save me. Yet I have to say something.

"There's blood." My voice trembles. "It's coming from his head."

Luca crooks a finger, beckoning me forward.

My heart drops.

I don't want to go to him, yet I'm drawn. Pulled. My feet creep closer of their own accord, then I'm crouching, succumbing to his silent command.

"Penny," Luther growls. "What are you doing?"

"His pulse… I-I'm checking his pulse."

What I'm really doing is staring into the eyes of the man who has fractured me. The one who fills me with relief because he's still alive. But there's no justification for my celebration, not when I'm responsible for his injuries, and his upcoming death.

"*I'm sorry.*" I break our visual connection in an attempt to sever my guilt and focus on the lengthy gash along the side of his head, the oozing blood matting his hair. I'm about to reach out, to sweep the strands away to inspect his wound when Cole curses, the violent outburst from the other side of my hiding place enough to make me retreat.

"Get his weapon," Luther demands of me. "Then unlock the door and hand it to Chris."

"Don't do it," Cole snarls. "Don't fucking do it, Penny."

My heart sinks as I glance to my left and find Luca's gun on the tile a few feet away.

There's no choice. With Luther armed and Chris waiting outside, evil has already prevailed.

Gentle fingers brush my wrist, stealing my attention. My focus. I meet Luca's gaze. I see the struggle to fight etched in his features—the tight lips, the drawn brows.

"*Don't,*" he mouths, begging me with his eyes. "*Don't do it.*"

For once, I want to please him. A criminal. A *man*. I'd give anything to grant his wish. Instead, I paste on a regretful smile, hoping he understands the apology that comes with it.

I should've told him what was happening when we were alone in the bedroom. I should've let down my guard and believed his promises. Then this situation might have ended differently.

But the bad guys always win.

"She does what she's told," Luther seethes. "Otherwise she knows the consequences."

I straighten, hearing the threat loud and clear.

"What's to stop her shooting you?" Cole asks.

"She could try. But she'd be dead before she had time to aim. And then I'd kill all her friends just to spite her."

That's why I have no choice. *That's* why I have to take Luca's gun.

I reach for the weapon a few feet away, my fingers tingling as my palm slides over the blood-slicked exterior. It's a strange sensation—touching a gun for the first time. The slightest ebb of power flows through me as I grip the cold metal in both hands.

If only I could shoot Luther. If I had the experience and skills to risk everything on a quick draw, I would.

Luca's hand reclaims my wrist, the fingers trailing slowly over my skin. "*Give it here,*" he mouths.

I want to. I want nothing more than to let him continue

to be the savior he promised to be. I just can't. I won't place my life in the hands of a stranger. Nor the lives of the women waiting for my return. Not when he's possible heartbeats away from death.

"I'm sorry." My lips form the silent words as remorse slaughters me from the inside out. "I've got the gun," I announce to the room and stand.

I forget about the man at my feet. I shut out the guilt and shame.

"Keep it," Cole slurs. "Don't give it to Chris."

"Don't even think about it." Luther jabs his son in the shoulder with his gun as if sensing an act of retaliation. "You're predictable. Always have been."

"Too bad you've already admitted you won't kill me, old man."

I ignore their squabbling and focus on what has to be done. Everything fades away as my bare feet trek the cool tile toward the glass door covered by a sheer curtain. I can already see Chris standing in wait on the other side. I can feel his darkness. Can predict more bloodshed.

"Tell Penny not to give him the gun and we can talk this out." Cole's words are garbled. "That's what you want, right? To show me the error of my ways?"

I shut him out. I shut *everything* out.

There's only the wild beat of my pulse and hollowness. An empty void carves its existence into my soul, preparing me for death.

I don't stop my progression toward the door. I don't pause even though the only option I have makes my heart stutter.

Life doesn't flash before my eyes—it blinks slowly. Snapshots of memories I've longed to forget assail me. I see my parents. My brothers. My friends. Everything drifts into my mind until I reach the curtain and pull it aside.

"Tell her to stop. *Do it.*" Cole raises his voice. "Penny. Don't. Don't be stupid."

The argument continues behind me. I'm sure the sound of a scuffle or a fight brushes my ears, but all I see is Chris. The cold stare. The conniving smirk.

His crimes come back to haunt me as I tighten the gun in my grip, yet there's no uncertainty in his expression. There's no doubt in his mind I'll hand over the weapon like a good little slave.

His opinion of me is humiliating.

The condescension. The superiority.

I unflick the lock and yank the door wide, the sea breeze kissing my cheeks while his smirk increases.

He doesn't rush me. He only provokes with his confident leer, waiting for me to comply to yet another demand. Even with a weapon drawn in his direction he's entirely certain I won't shoot him. How could I when a lifetime of conditioning has ensured I'll obey?

"*No,*" Cole yells, the protest ringing in my ears.

I don't want to do this. I'm scared. Nauseous.

I raise the gun in both hands, slowly inching it toward my enemy, the aim creeping from his feet, along his legs, to his stomach.

The more dire my aim, the more Chris smirks.

"That's a good pretty Penny," he drawls, the taunt barely audible yet deeply unsettling.

Cole shouts another protest. There's another scuffle of feet. Then a warning from Luther.

A million rampant heartbeats pass and still the smirk

beaming back at me doesn't falter. Not until I force myself to smile back, my lips slowly lifting in a mirrored taunt.

For a second, the most beautiful sight of trepidation blinks back at me. All it takes is a squeeze of the trigger to cement his fear in place.

Pop. Pop.

My arms shake with the blasts. My ears ring.

Chris jolts with both impacts, his eyes widening, his skin turning pale as a lake of red seeps from the holes in his shirt.

His descent is fluid, almost beautiful, as he falls backward, sailing through the air until his head hits the cement tile with a deafening crack.

Pride rushes through me as the gun slides from my fingers and a sob of achievement escapes my throat.

"I'll fucking kill you," Luther roars.

Yes, he will. That outcome was always blindingly obvious.

I close my eyes, raise my face to the dawning sun, and wait for piercing bullets to take my life.

"Get down," Cole yells. "*Hide.*"

I don't move. I crave the anticipated peace. I want the freedom of death.

"I've got her."

There's more scuffling. Footsteps patter behind me. But that voice. It wasn't Cole. Or Luther.

I spin. Luca charges toward me, his face stricken, the barrel of Luther's gun quickly trekking his movements.

I open my mouth, a scream of warning about to launch from my throat.

Pop. Pop.

Luca slams into me and we fall backward, hitting the floor with enough force to wind me.

Shouts rain. A frenzy of movement ensues. But all I can do is gasp for air as I'm dragged behind the kitchen island counter and propped against the cupboards.

"Are you okay?" He crouches before me, his blood-covered hands roaming my face, shoulders, arms. "Were you shot?"

I shake my head as I struggle for breath.

The side of his head drips with crimson, the rivulets descending from his hairline as he continues to search me, his gaze stopping at my cream pants now splattered with red.

"It's yours," I murmur. "I'm not hurt."

That penetrating gaze returns to mine, his intensity adding to the whir of adrenaline intoxicating my system.

"It's not my blood," I repeat. "I'm fine."

He nods, the movement laced with a wince, then pivots toward the danger, his back to me as he raises one leg of his jeans and retrieves a knife from a sheath attached to his ankle.

"It's over, Dad. Your new protege failed to inject me properly," Cole mumbles the words. "Your dog is dead. And you fucked up when you thought you took Luca out."

"You forget I'm the only one with a weapon, son."

I inch farther back into my hiding place, completely aware of Luther's power.

He's got the gun. He isn't injured. He's in control.

"I'm sorry, motherfucker, but you're mistaken."

A woman's voice catches me off guard as she walks inside through the open glass doors.

She has to be the little fox.

She clutches a gun in her hands, her shoulders high and strong, her face hardened like a warrior's. "Lower the weapon, Luther. Hand it over and this may not have to end badly."

I need to help her. I have to stop hiding like a child and grab the gun I dropped. I can run. Sprint. Slide and snatch.

Luca glances over his shoulder at me and mouths, "*Get back.*"

I shake my head and jut my chin in the direction of my weapon.

"*Get back,*" he repeats, his arm reaching out to guide me into submission.

He ignores my plan—ignores me in general—as he creeps closer to the edge of our island hiding place and sneaks a peek around the cupboards.

"Don't shoot, Nis," Cole demands. "He won't kill me."

Luther won't kill him? Is he kidding?

I fumble onto my haunches, preparing to make a run for salvation as Luther drawls out a pithy insult. I either want to die in a rain of bullets or be completely freed. I won't sit by as the devil regains the upper hand so he can draw out my punishment for days.

Weeks.

Months.

I'm about to make a run for it when Luca lunges for me, his trunk of an arm tackling me around the waist to haul me back into him.

I fight his hold as he drags me between his legs, his thighs closing in around me, the knife clutched in his free hand.

"Quit it," he growls low in my ear, his voice barely

audible over the threats and demands being continuously flung around the armed standoff. "Cole needs to finish this. It's his right. Otherwise I would've already done it myself."

I shake my head, denying his words and the voices screaming in my skull.

My instincts demand I take action.

"Don't be scared," he whispers. "Trust me."

I keep shaking my head, over and over, trying to drown out the mania.

I'm going to be tied to a table. I'll be brutalized by anyone and everyone who enters Luther's house.

"He's safe, Anissa," Luca speaks louder. "Give Cole your gun and let him finish this."

I struggle to focus on the conversation. Who's safe? Cole? Tobias?

Doesn't Luca realize nobody is free from harm when Luther is armed?

I wiggle, attempting to break free of his strong hold but Luca grips me tighter, hugging my back to his chest.

"I've got you," he murmurs. "Just drown it out. This will be over soon."

I try. I concentrate so hard on escaping to my mental sanctuary. I hide in silence, in darkness, and still the panic finds me.

Cole's slurred words brush the edge of my consciousness.

The woman's demands haunt me.

Then Luca speaks up. "I'm not hiding, asshole. I'm giving Cole space to finish this his way. And if he can't, I'm on standby with a knife in my hand, ready and willing to slit your throat."

There's so much vehemence in his tone. A wealth of determined conviction.

I want to believe him.

I can picture this man sinking his blade into my enemy's neck. But he won't. He can't.

Not when Luther always wins.

Evil. Always. Conquers.

Luca holds me tighter. I can't stop fighting and I'm not sure if it's because I want to escape his touch or I fear he'll soon be killed if I don't act.

It's too much.

It's all too much.

"Give him your gun." Luca waves at the woman. "Let him finish this."

No. *No.*

I rock harder, willing the madness away. Begging for my life to be over.

I can't go back. I won't.

The woman steps out of view and I sense a change in the air. The tension builds around us.

"Cole, I'm going to shoot," she announces. "I can't let him take another step."

Luther must be close. Almost within range of the island counter.

Luca loosens his hold and slides out from behind me, his weapon at the ready, his body crouching lower as if preparing for battle.

I need to fight.

I can't hide. I can't show weakness. But that's what my potential savior is asking of me—to remain vulnerable. To cower.

I slide back to the wall, bow my head and jam my

fingers into my ears. It's all I can do to stop myself from running for that gun when everything inside me is screaming to *fight, fight, fight.*

I rock on my haunches like a child. I pretend it's only a matter of time before Luther is taken down, when in reality I know he's seconds away from killing this woman… then his adult son… followed by the man at my side… then me.

"Stop. *Luther. Stop,*" she yells. "Release the gun or I'll shoot."

I can still hear her. The panic. The fear.

I rock harder. Faster.

"Cole?" the woman pleads.

I can feel Luther behind me. It's as if he's right there, peering down, the whole world entirely still. Only me and him. Power pitted against instability.

Pop.

I jerk backward at the sudden blast, my ears ringing, my head filling with static.

Luca rushes to his feet and I frantically scramble to follow, both of us joining the woman who stands tall, and Cole who is hunched on the tile, as we stare at Luther laid flat on the floor.

Blood seeps from his mouth as he gurgles and splutters, the gun remaining tight in his grip.

My tormentor continues to breathe, his chest rising and falling while the barrel of his weapon slowly edges its way toward his son.

He's going to shoot. He's going to—

Pop.

Pop.

I jump with the explosions.

Pop.

Pop.

Anissa keeps shooting, over and over until the wild bursts of noise resemble hollow clicks and the man who stole my life stares blankly ahead. Not breathing. Not blinking.

Dead.

I always anticipated blinding happiness when I fantasized about this moment. I thought I'd want to laugh. To dance. To celebrate.

None of the jubilation hits me.

There's no bliss. Not even peace.

I'm still hollow.

Empty.

Until Tobias's sweet voice calls from the hall. "Baba? *Baba?*"

7

LUCA

I KEEP SEEING HER. THE FRANTIC RUSH ACROSS THE ROOM. The desperate way she scooped the kid into her arms and carried him into the hall.

I thought about nothing but Penny as Cole and I loaded the dead bodies onto Luther's boat. I escorted those fuckers out to sea while Cole tailed me in another vessel.

It wasn't hard to dispose of the evidence.

I weighed down the cadavers and threw them overboard, keeping watch until they sank from view. Then I gave Cole instructions on how to rig his father's boat to drive unaided, because my head throbbed so much I couldn't fucking do it myself.

Even now, as I clean my own blood off the living room wall, my brain protests every movement. It feels like I'm one sneeze away from an aneurism. Or a fucking stroke.

And still, Penny plagues my thoughts. She's been left alone for too long. Both her *and* the kid. The only reason I know they haven't attempted escape is because the sound of a sniffling child continues to echo down the hall.

"When are you going to speak to the boy?" I ask Cole.

He stops scrubbing the crimson splotches on the floor and leans back on his haunches. "I'm not sure. I thought it might be better to wait until his father's insides are cleaned off the tile."

I grate my teeth at his sarcasm. "The longer you leave it, the harder it will be."

"Then you go." He jerks his chin at me. "Play the hero. Go beat your chest and attempt to win over Decker's sister. See how far it gets you."

I ignore the derision and scrub harder, the pungent scent of bleach searing my nostrils.

This isn't about me 'playing the hero.'

She's been through hell, not only today, but for God knows how long. She's fragile. Temperamental. Volatile.

From the way she rocked behind the kitchen counter, I'd say she's one gentle gush of wind away from crumpling like a deck of cards.

It's in our best interest to keep an eye on her.

"Go on, Captain America," Cole drawls. "Save her from isolation."

Fuck it.

Fuck him.

He's been a major asshole since his father's murder, and I get it, the situation didn't end how he anticipated. He didn't take out the head of his family. A woman did. A Fed.

He made the mistake of sleeping with the enemy who swept the victory out from underneath him. But that's not my fault. I'd warned him about getting close to Anissa.

"Fine." I throw my cloth to the floor. "I will."

I stalk for the hall and follow the sound of a sniffing child all the way to my bedroom door. And there they are, huddled on the floor beneath the windowsill, Tobias snuggled in Penny's tight embrace.

As soon as I breach the threshold she stiffens, her panicked gaze meeting mine.

"It's okay." I creep inside the room. "I just wanted to see how you two are holding up."

The boy eyes me as if I'm his worst nightmare, his arms clutched around Penny's middle, his legs curled close to hers.

"We're dealing the best we can." She runs a hand through Tobias's hair, her mothering entirely natural.

"Can I get you anything? Food? Something to drink?"

Her gaze slowly treks me—from my face, all the way down to my hands. I do the same, taking in the blood splatter. Death stains every inch of me. My clothes. My skin. Some dried and cracking, other parts remaining liquified.

"I probably should've taken a quick look in the mirror before I came in."

She winces in agreement. "What's going on out there?"

I slowly inch to the bed and sit on the corner farthest from them, attempting a laidback demeanor. "We're just finishing the clean-up."

"What about the other woman? Is she still with you?"

"Anissa? No." I tread lightly in the hope Penny won't repeat information she never should've been privy to. "She's outside, clearing her head."

More accurately, I escorted her from the house because Cole couldn't stand to look at her. I'm sure she's down at the pier by now, impatiently waiting for a ticket out of here.

"I'd like to speak to her."

"Maybe later. For now, it's best if we all keep our distance. It's been a long morning."

She falls quiet, her dark eyes filling with questions. "Can you at least tell me what happens next?"

"In terms of a detailed schedule, I have no idea." I shrug. "But you're not a prisoner, if that's what you're asking."

She sucks in a breath and straightens. "Good. Because I'd like to leave as soon as possible."

"Yeah, I get it. I'd be eager to get home, too. But it's going to take time. We're waiting on a jet—"

"No, I don't mean going home to the States. I'm talking about Luther's house. I need to get back there."

"What?" I push to my feet and she scrambles to do the same, panicked caution flooding her features.

"We need to leave." She drags Tobias to stand alongside her. "We have to get back to my sisters."

She straightens to her full height like a mighty warrior climbing from the pits of hell. But her invisible armor is flimsy at best. The bravado she exudes is fake. I can see under the facade to the frightened woman beneath.

I shake my head and mentally curse the resulting thud of my brain. "That's not an option."

"So I *am* a prisoner?" she rasps.

I massage my temples, attempting to alleviate the quickly building stroke. "If we're talking about being captive to your own stupidity, then yeah, I guess you're a prisoner. Because there's no way in hell you're leaving here until it's safe."

Her nostrils flare as I witness the little trust I'd gained flitter away with every spite-filled blink of her eyes.

"Look." I lower a hand from my temple, raising it, palm up, in peace. "It's not rational for you to be anywhere but here."

"It's not safe for my family if I stay." She starts for the door, Tobias tagging along at her side.

"Your family?" I stalk ahead and block their path. "I can assure you, they're fine. In fact, your brother is on his way here as we speak."

She stops, her eyes flaring, her gentle lips parted. Then the shock is hidden behind another firm squaring of her shoulders. "I don't have a brother."

Jesus Christ.

Not this shit again.

"Are you kidding me?"

"No, I'm not kidding you," she grates. "The only family I have are the women living in Luther's mansion, the ones who are fearing for my safety. The ones who are currently under more threat than I've ever been."

"They'll be okay. Cole will pull some strings and make sure they're taken care of."

"What strings?" Her question is flung like an accusation. "There are no strings when it comes to Luther's operation. The police won't help you. The locals won't either. Dead or not, Luther is still entirely in control, which means they're sitting ducks unless I can get to them."

The kid lets out a big sniffle, the sound shooting into my skull like another motherfucking bullet. I'm dying here. Slowly succumbing to the mental torment.

"I said we'd handle it." I return to massaging my temples. "You can trust me."

"I can trust you?" She frowns with incredulity. "The man who claims I'm not a prisoner, yet refuses to let me leave?"

Maybe if my brain wasn't currently being shoved through a grater I'd admire her tenacity, but this shit is getting old. For starters, Cole would never let her sail away from here with his half-brother. Not when she's not the kid's mother. She hasn't been missing long enough to carry the same blood as the child.

"I'm going to call your brother." I don't want to spoil the reunion. As far as Decker is concerned, his sister is dead. But I'm clutching at straws here. I don't know how else to get her to back down apart from pulling the cell from my jeans pocket. "You can speak to him for yourself. He can reassure you I'm trustworthy."

"No."

I dial his number anyway.

"I said *no*." Her expression turns frantic. Wide eyes. Pale skin. She's more scared now than when she was trying to jab me in the neck with a fucking syringe. "Turn it off."

I don't.

Instead, I switch the phone to speaker, the loud ring torture to my ears. "He thought he lost you a long time ago—"

"I said *turn it off*." She snatches for the device, attempting to claw it from my hand.

"What the fuck is wrong with you?" I hold the phone out of reach, the ringing continuing. "I thought you'd be excited to speak to family after all this time."

"I don't have a family." Her breathing becomes ragged.

"Not back there. Not in the States. The only family I have is here."

She grabs at my arms, trying to get hold of the device, but the moment the call connects she freezes, her entire body turned to stone.

"This is me." Decker's voice fills the room. "Leave a message."

I bring the phone toward her as the answering service releases a high-pitched beep.

She doesn't speak. All she does is stare at the cell framed in my blood-stained hand.

"Are you going to say something?" I inch the phone closer.

She shakes her head, still staring.

Fucking hell.

I disconnect the call and place the device back in my jeans pocket.

"He's on his way." I lower my voice, trying like hell to comfort her as she wages a war behind those stricken eyes. "You're going to see him any minute now."

"No." She steps back, taking the kid with her. "I don't want to see him."

She's in shock. Fight or flight. Or any number of fucked up mental challenges associated with the shit storm she's been through. But she's on the home straight now. This is where her healing begins.

"It's okay." I reach for her, not sure what the fuck I'm doing. "You're safe."

"No." She slinks away from my touch, backtracking again and again. "*No.*"

Fuck.

She's crumpling and that kid is about to go down with her if she doesn't pull up from the nose-dive.

"Penny, you're safe." I follow her, getting close to make sure she can hear, see, and feel my sincerity. "Robert, Chris, and Luther are gone. All the shit you've been through is over. And I swear on my own brother's life I'm going to get you home."

She shakes her head faster and faster, her breathing fractured as she stares right through me.

"I've got you." I reach out again, attempting to calm her with a touch. "It's going to be—"

"*No*." She scoots away. "I don't want to see him. I don't want to see any of them. I just want to leave."

I let her place space between us, taking it as a win that she's finally acknowledged her brother, no matter how minimal the admission.

"Penny…" Tobias tangles his fingers in her blouse, pulling the material down until he's close to popping a button. "I'm scared."

Her hyperventilating lessens.

Everything dilutes—the shaking of her head, the blink of fear-filled eyes. She reins in her crazy for the boy's sake.

"I'm sorry." She pivots to him, engulfing his shoulders in her arms to pull him tight against her. "There's no need to be scared. I'm just a little…"

"Overwhelmed?" I offer.

She winces and follows it up with a nod. "He's right. I'm overwhelmed."

"Is he still a bad man?" the kid mumbles, looking at me from his shielded position against her side. "Dad said he was telling Cole bad things."

Great. Fucking great.

I turn my attention to Penny and raise a brow. I'm not touching the kid's question with a ten-foot pole. One, because he sure as shit won't believe me. And two, because I have no idea what the fuck his scumbag father told him.

"We're going to be okay." She runs a hand through his hair, the placation timid at best. "Luca is trying to help us."

Trying?

My fucking ass I'm trying.

I conquered that bullshit when I risked my life to run through a spray of bullets and tackle her to safety.

We both know I mastered that motherfucker like a pro, but I don't have the focus or patience to point out the obvious.

"I'm going to leave you two alone." I hold tight for a few seconds, waiting for her to protest. Waiting for anything.

When she doesn't speak, I give up and back away. "I'll be in the living room. Call out if you need me."

Still, she doesn't react. All she does is continue to taunt my need to win her over.

I don't understand my obsession with earning her trust. But it's there, clawing its way under my skin.

It isn't until I reach the door that she breaks the silence.

"Luca." My name is gentle on her lips. "They don't have a lot of time."

"They?" I pause, not turning to face her.

There's a squeak of my mattress. She's on my fucking bed. "The women—my sisters. They aren't safe. Luther had plans to ensure we're never freed."

I remain in place, forcing myself not to imagine her

sliding between my sheets. "How much time are we talkin' about?"

"I don't know."

"Okay." I nod, my back still facing her. "I'll take care of it."

God only knows how, but I will.

I leave them in the bedroom, my boots thudding down the hall, then into the living room where I find Cole still on his hands and knees on the bloodstained tiles.

"Have fun?" he asks.

"Yeah. A whole heap." I snatch my cloth from the floor and return to the gore plastered on the wall. "Just so you know, she's itching to get away from here. She says those women at your dad's house are under threat."

"I don't doubt it," he grates. "But we've got more important issues to deal with. Keira is already on the water. She'll be here any minute."

I pause my circular scrub. "Then I should also point out that Penny isn't doing cartwheels at the thought of seeing her brother, either."

He sits up straighter and cocks his ear toward the glass doors. "Well, that's too bad, because I can already hear their boat."

8

PENNY

I encourage Tobias onto the bed and begin to pace.

Luca had repeatedly referred to one of my brothers, never mentioning which of the two he was in contact with. Then he'd placed the call and the answering message had kicked in.

The familiar voice had collided with my skepticism, smashing it to smithereens.

Sebastian—the youngest of my two older siblings. The one who kept the high school bullies at bay. The playful jokester.

He has ties to Luca? He's on his way here?

"What's wrong?" Tobias pulls his knees to his chest and cuddles his legs. "What's happening?"

"Nothing." I stop mid-pace. "I'm just thinking."

"About Nina and Lilly?"

"Yes." I paste on a smile. "Abi and Chloe, too. We need to get back to them. It's really important."

He nods, not a moment of hesitation. "I don't want to stay here."

"Me either. And we won't. Not for long. But we might have to be a little sneaky to make sure we leave as soon as possible. Do you think you can handle that?"

"I'm always sneak—"

I hold up a hand, silencing him at the rumble of sound approaching the island. It's a boat. The grumble grows louder and louder.

My chest tightens. Arrhythmia takes over.

If that's Sebastian… if my brother is actually here…

A curdled mix of emotions strangle my insides—excitement, apprehension, impatience, fear.

I rush to the door and tilt my head to hear Luca and Cole's conversation. They're arguing about Anissa and when she should be sent home.

I hear the monotonous scrape of cleaning. The increased rumble from the boat. The building pound in my ears. Then the engine is cut and the fading gurgle makes me nauseous with indecision.

I itch to run for a brother that might be here to save me, yet I should hide from him, too.

I need him, and I have to stay away.

I can't fall victim to weakness now. Not when my battle is far from over. Those women in Luther's house are my top priority and succumbing to the allure of a savior won't help any of us.

A door whooshes open in the distance. An unfamiliar woman's voice rings out. And another. More men, too. But none I recognize.

I begin to sag with pained relief that my brother isn't here when a cocky voice enters the mix.

"I'm told I have some secret present waiting for me."

I suck in a ragged breath.

It's him.

Sebastian.

My blood surges. My heart pounds.

I'm torn. Broken in two. It's killing me not knowing if I should knock down my walls or build them higher. Keep battling or finally embrace vulnerability.

Every limb trembles with the need to surrender. I want, want, *want* my demons slain for me. It's all I yearn for. Yet I can't count on anyone. Not even a brother I previously would've entrusted with my life.

I back away from the door, letting longing slowly slip through my fingers.

"We need to get out of here, little guy." I paste on a smile and turn to Tobias still sitting on the bed. "Are you ready for an adventure?"

"Where are we going? Will we take Baba's boat back to Naxos?"

"Maybe. Do you know how to drive a boat?" I make the question light-hearted even though I seriously have no idea how we're going to get off this island. I'm not sure I'd even know how to drive a car anymore, let alone a boat.

He gives me a sheepish grin, the first pleasure-filled expression he's shown since this morning. "A little. Baba would let me steer the wheel sometimes."

"That's perfect."

It's entirely *not* perfect, but I'll figure it out.

If we can escape without being noticed maybe I can wave down a fisherman or some tourists. Someone has to be on the water nearby.

I help Tobias from the bed and lead him to the window. "We're going to climb out." I grip the frame, about to pull the window open when I notice the motion sensors attached to the glass.

Goddammit.

"What's wrong?" Tobias asks. "Do you need my help to lift it?"

My heart clenches at his sweetness. "No. It's okay. But maybe going out the window isn't the best idea."

I need to think.

Think. Think. Think.

My brain fails me, my concentration continuously returning to the mumbled words carrying from the living room.

"Penny?" Tobias grips my blouse. "I need to use the bathroom."

Shit.

"Can you hold on? Just for a little while?"

He winces. "I don't know."

"Where. The fuck. Is she?" My brother bellows from the living room.

He knows.

He's been told I'm alive.

I swing around, searching for another way of escape. I can't see him. Fragility already chips away at my bones.

"Penny?" Tobias tugs my blouse. "I'm scared."

I exhale a pained breath.

Think. Think. Think.

Pounding footsteps approach, the thunder echoing inside my chest, the noise adding to the thud of my pulse.

Then everything stops as if the world was carried away on the breeze.

There's no sound. No movement. Only the skitter of

awareness at the back of my neck that tells me we're no longer alone.

"Penny?"

This time my name isn't spoken by Tobias.

It's *him*. The man I've fought not to think about for months on end.

I tremble. Everywhere.

It's hard to breathe as I turn and meet Sebastian's stare in the doorway.

Sweet relief floods my system, drowning me in happiness. *Weakness.*

I raise my chin to the threat. Square my shoulders and force myself not to break.

"Penny?" he repeats, his forehead wrinkled in anguish.

He's older now, his bright eyes dull, his full smile non-existent. The man standing in the doorway has been hardened from the joyful young adult I remember.

I'm not sure I know this man and I'm certain he no longer knows me.

Tobias tugs my blouse again and whispers my name.

"It's okay, Toby." I clear the emotion from my throat but can't stop myself from guiding him to move behind me. "There's nothing to fear."

It's a lie.

I used to dream of this reunion. I'd picture how I would run to Sebastian once he'd saved me from this horror. I'd cry. He'd cry. Mom, Dad, and my older brother, Graham, would be there, too.

But those thoughts were merely fantasies when my captor made certain I would never be free.

I fear for my safety like never before. I'm scared this

man will blind me to reality. That I'll get washed up in the reunion I've longed for and forget that Luther has a plan for me that won't end even though he's dead.

"Oh, God, I can't believe you're alive." Sebastian rushes forward.

I panic. Full-blown hysteria takes over.

"*Stop*." I scramble backward, shielding Tobias behind me, one hand on his shoulder, the other stretched out in front of me in warning. "Stay where you are."

My brother freezes. "Penny, it's me." His voice is filled with rejection. And the way he looks at me. *God.* I can't take it.

I don't know how he got mixed up with Luca and Cole. I'm not sure I want to know. But I can't join him.

My sisters are still in danger. My *new family* need my help. And I won't be anything other than worthless if I let my brother take one step closer to my temperamental stability.

"I don't want to see you." I backtrack, inching closer to the window.

He jerks as if my words hit him like a physical blow.

I can't take the guilt. His sorrow strips layers from me —his judgment at who I've become slices deep.

"Please leave." I hold his stare, not softening the harshness of my expression. "Now."

His lips part. Shoulders slump. "I…"

Luca appears in the doorway, infusing me with relief.

"Get him out of here," I beg. "*Please.*"

"Don't panic." Luca edges into the room, stopping beside Sebastian. "You've got nothing to worry about."

I have *everything* to worry about—my brothers' safety,

and that of my parents. I don't want any of them near me. Not now. Not ever.

"Make him leave." I creep closer and closer to the window.

"I will, I promise, but you need to tell me why."

I shake my head. I don't need to tell him anything. Not when my trust in him bounces like a rubber ball. One minute he's my savior, the next my captor.

"What the hell is going on?" Sebastian murmurs. "Why is she scared of me?"

The answer clogs my throat, the words filled with far too much depth and destruction for anyone to understand. Nobody here is capable of comprehending my fear over what I could do to him. What the dangers surrounding me will bring.

I just want to go back to pretending my family doesn't exist. My meager strength was far less brittle then.

Luca doesn't quit holding my gaze. He keeps the visual connection steady, not judging, not sympathizing. Just strong.

"Penny, Decker has put his life on the line for a long time all in an effort to find you."

I continue to back away, not wanting to hear the placations.

"He didn't willingly begin working with Cole," he continues. "It was all for you."

"You work for Cole?" I pin my brother with a stare, my insides begging for him to deny the betrayal. "You work for the family who took me?"

"It's not like that." He shakes his head. "It's complicated."

"We didn't know." A woman inches into the room. "We had no idea what was happening in Greece."

I cast my gaze over her, from the gleaming shoes, to the designer clothes, all the way up to her subtly perfect make-up. She's beautiful. But there's something about her that sets me on edge. A familiarity. "Who are you?"

"Keira." She gives a sad smile. "I'm Cole's sister. And I'm told this little guy is my half-brother." Her smile increases as she looks at Tobias. "It's an honor to meet you."

The hair on the back of my neck prickles.

The familiarity makes sense now. She's Luther's daughter. She even has the devil's eyes. His full lips, too.

"Get them out of here," I demand of Luca. "Or give me a way off this island. *Now.*"

Tobias trembles behind me, the tremors of his body sinking into mine.

"Penny." Luca's voice is smooth. "You're not a prisoner here. You can both move around freely—get something to eat, have a shower, get changed, sleep if you want. But it's not safe to leave."

"I can look after myself."

"Can you?" He raises a brow. "All on your own? Without the kid? Because there's no way in hell Torian will let you leave with his brother."

I don't react to the threat.

I knew Tobias would be their invisible shackle. Yet the delivery of the blow still leaves a gaping wound. "So he's the prisoner now?"

"No." Luca takes another step. "There are no prisoners. The kid is Torian's brother. He's family. You have no right to take him."

"I have every right. I'm the only parental figure he has left. I'm his teacher. His friend. His cook. His maid. I'm the one who tucks him in at night."

"Penny." Tobias clings tighter to me. "Please don't leave me." His heartbreaking kiddy sniffles return.

"You would take him from me after everything he's witnessed today? After all the stories he's been told?" I beg Luca with my eyes when I'd prefer to glare. Claw. Retaliate. "Can you imagine what he's thinking right now? Luther told him you were the enemy. He was forced to attack Cole. Now you want to take him from the only familiarity he has left?"

Toby's trembles increase, adding fuel to my argument.

"I'm not the enemy." The woman crouches. "Tobias, I would never do anything to hurt you. We're family."

Her words are gentle. The delivery soft. She's trying to win him over, bit by bit, second by second.

"You can attempt to brainwash him all you want," I snip. "Believe me, he's grown accustomed to the family trait, but he still can't stay here. He needs his medicine."

"What medicine?" Luca demands.

"He's diabetic." I squeeze Tobias's shoulder and hope to hell he realizes it's a sign for him to keep his mouth shut. "He needs regular injections. If I don't get him home soon he'll get sick. He could die."

Keira stands, her attention swaying from Sebastian to Luca and back again. "We need to tell Cole."

"Wait." Luca's eyes narrow on me. "The kid is diabetic?"

I swallow, suddenly unsettled with the thought of pinning more attention on Tobias.

"I assume there are risks associated with taking them back to Dad's house," Keira adds.

Dad.

God, the parental term when referencing Luther is abhorrent. He was never a father. Only a monster.

"The risks are monumental," Luca growls, his focus turning harsh. "They're not going back there."

I stand taller. "Do you plan on forcibly stopping me?"

"You bet I do."

"Luca," Sebastian warns. "Watch yourself."

My heart squeezes at the protection. Squeezes then flounders.

I remain locked tight in a visual battle with Luca, his scrutiny scathing as he attempts to stare me down.

"We need to talk," he tells me. "In private."

"Like hell you do." Sebastian steps closer. "I'm not leaving you alone with her."

Luca doesn't falter. He keeps his eyes narrowed on mine. "Now," he speaks to me.

I don't know what this is about. But I can see the determination in his expression. Whatever it is holds importance.

"Leave us," I murmur.

"That's not going to happen." Sebastian crosses his arms over his chest. "I'll never let you out of my sight again."

My heart protests the protection, wanting it and rejecting it at the same time.

"Get out." I raise my voice. "I don't want you here."

Pain seeps into his features, tainting everything it touches—his eyes, his lips.

"And take the kid," Luca adds.

"What?" I grasp Tobias's shoulders. "*No.*"

"It's only for a few minutes. Keira can get him something to eat."

The woman nods. "I'll look after him."

I glare at her—the daughter to my rapist, the blood of my nightmares.

"Nothing is going to happen to him," Luca continues. "He's with family here."

"I don't like this," Sebastian growls. "I want to know what the hell is going on."

The room falls silent waiting for me to make the next move. I don't know what to do—succumb to my brother, give Luca what he wants, or forge ahead with my demand to leave.

Every option has pitfalls, but none more so than my lack of confidence to get off this island alone or my fear at dragging my brother into a mess he won't survive.

That leaves Luca.

"Let us talk in private." I glance away, wanting the surly man to know I'm not happily obliging to his request.

There's more silence, where I feel my brother's wince instead of seeing it. His disappointment ebbs through the room, dirtying my skin.

"If you need anything," he bites out, "you fucking yell, okay? Scream and I'll be back in here to kill this motherfucker before he can take another breath."

I don't show my appreciation. I can't. Letting my guard down and thanking him isn't something I can come back from. Instead, I turn to crouch before Tobias, yet again pasting on a dishonest smile.

"I don't want to go," he starts. "I want to stay with you."

"I know. But you're going to be fine." I pray I'm not lying to him. I beg the heavens to grant me this one favor. "It's only for a few minutes."

"You promise?"

"Of course I do. I'd never put you in harm's way. You know that." I grab his hands. "Go. Get some food. Take a look around."

"But—"

"It's time to listen, Tobias. This is important. Remember what I said about getting back home?"

He nods, his face pinched with understanding.

"Good." I squeeze his fingers. "We need to get the others. And to do that I have to talk to Luca."

He sinks his teeth into his lower lip as if fighting off the need to disobey.

"It's only a few minutes," I repeat. "Find me something to eat."

"Come on, kiddo." Sebastian's voice is filled with reluctance. "Neither one of us want to leave her, so let's do it together."

I ignore the ache in my heart and lean forward to whisper in Toby's ear. "Don't answer any questions. Don't tell them anything."

He wraps his arms around me, clinging tight as if we're about to be separated for months instead of moments. "I'll be smart."

"I know you will." I pull back and give him a quick kiss on the forehead. "Go."

He holds his head high as he walks toward the strangers, Keira reaching out a hand he refuses to take.

That little boy has a wealth of fortitude. With his upbringing, he had no choice. Violence has been an everyday occurrence. He was raised on a steady diet of brutality.

He hasn't even cried over his father's death—there have only been a million sniffles to hold the emotion at bay. He will break, though. Once he feels safe he'll temporarily slip into the child he's meant to be, letting the heartache free before he becomes the product of his emotionless father all over again.

"We'll be back soon." Sebastian starts for the door. "And we're not going far."

They leave together, each member of the trio taking turns in glancing over their shoulder with uncertainty before Luca closes the door behind them, trapping me in the room with him.

I try not to falter. To panic at the isolation with this formidable man.

"It's not a good idea to lie." He turns to face me, his eyes squinted in judgment. "So let's pretend it didn't happen."

"Excuse me?" I swallow over the building tension. This man is nothing in comparison to Luther, or even Chris or Robert. But he's devoid of innocence, too. There's something about him that niggles at my self-preservation.

"We both know that kid isn't diabetic."

I hold his stare, neither confirming nor denying his keen assessment.

"He hasn't had food or water for a damn long time," he drawls, "I'm sure he'd be showing symptoms by now."

Still I don't respond.

"But I get it." He approaches in a lazy stride. Cool. Confident. Blood still painted down one cheek. The gash on the side of his head still glistening. "You're scared. You're grasping at straws to get your friends to safety."

"My *family*," I correct.

He inclines his head with a wince. "Yes. Your family. Those women. I'd do whatever it takes, too. But lying isn't going to help you. If you lead Torian into a bloodbath based on bullshit you're not going to like how he retaliates."

I step back at the warning. "You're threatening me?"

"I'm protecting you," he snarls. "You won't get what you want if you base your plea on lies. I told you I would take care of it."

"Yes, you told me you'd take care of it, with no understanding of the situation you're facing or the looming deadline. If we're going to be telling each other the truth, the least you can do is admit you were fobbing me off."

"No, I wasn't. I was only attempting to clean up one fucking mess before I took on another." He pinches the bridge of his nose and squeezes his eyes shut.

For a moment, I'm struck by his show of vulnerability.

He's hurting.

I haven't seen weakness from a man since I was taken by Luther long ago. It's always been strong men with stronger fists. And yes, this man remains strong, but there's a sense of honesty about him, too.

"I made a promise," he grates. "I don't do that lightly."

"You've made many promises. Including setting me free."

His eyes open slightly, narrowed slits staring back at me. "You *are* free."

My yearning to believe him hasn't lessened. Neither has the determination not to trust him.

"I'll help those women," he continues. "Have faith I can get them out."

"You won't make it through the front gates without me."

"Then I'm happy for you to provide the necessary insight that helps us to get in another way."

"Us?" I ignore yet another refusal to let me leave and focus on obtaining more information about his plan.

"I'm not stupid enough to go on my own. Your brother will want to help, and Hunter is always looking for a bit of fun."

Fun? *Fun.*

"Wrong choice of words." He drops his hand from his nose and holds it up to me in placation. "I meant Hunter enjoys retribution. Especially against those who deserve a lot of it. Your tormentors will pay for what they've done."

"I don't care about revenge. All I want are my sis—"

There's a tentative knock at the door.

"Yeah?" Luca snaps.

The barrier to the rest of the world opens, Tobias's little face coming into view. He rushes toward me, keeping his distance from Luca as he passes to hold up a cookie.

"This is for you," he offers. "They said you need to eat."

"Thank you." I grasp the offering but can't stomach taking a bite, not with the lives of four people riding on my negotiating skills.

"Penny?" Tobias cringes and twists his legs together. "I really need to use the bathroom now."

Shit.

I glance at Luca in question.

"It's right in here, little buddy." He jerks his head at the ajar door across the other side of the room, then quickly squeezes his eyes shut again, wincing. "Walk through the robe to the door at the end."

Tobias peers up at me, waiting for approval.

"It's okay." I want to go with him, to lessen his fear, but I'm not finished with Luca. Not by a long shot. "Freshen up while you're in there. Wash your face and hands."

He nods, keeping an eye on the stranger as he walks to the door before disappearing inside.

The conversation doesn't fall back into place once we're alone.

Luca's eyes remain partially squinted, his face pinched with discomfort.

Despite being uncertain about where to lay my trust, I don't like seeing him in pain.

"Do you need a doctor?"

"I'll be fine. It's nothing but a headache."

"It's not fine. Not when you expect me to entrust you with the lives of the people I love."

His nostrils flare. "You know what? The slightest bit of appreciation would go a long fucking way to ease the throb in my head. All I've done is try to help you and you keep spitting it back in my face."

I straighten, the tiniest fissure of regret breaking through my defenses.

He's right. I've shown very little thanks for what he's done. But that's because his promises of freedom don't feel real. The death of my captors seems like a dream.

Shock hasn't allowed for anything positive to sink in. Not relief or happiness.

Definitely not the appreciation he craves.

"I'm sorry," I whisper. "I'm not ungrateful. I'm just..."

"Forget it." He huffs out a sigh. "I've got a spare shirt if you want to get out of your stained clothes." His attention treks my body, the scrutiny far more subtle than what I'm used to. There's no desire. No threat. "Or Keira might have something you can borrow."

"I don't want anything from her." Not clothes. Not placations. "I'll make do with what I have."

"You can't go back to Naxos in bloodstained clothes."

I straighten. "Go back?"

"That's what you want, isn't it?" He raises a brow. "And apparently I can't get through the gates without you."

The appreciation he's been searching for finally hits me, the buzz filtering through my limbs. "Thank you."

"Don't thank me yet. Torian has to—"

"Penny." Tobias's frantic voice calls from the bathroom. "*Penny.*"

My heart drops, the cookie falling from my fingers.

I run, scrambling toward the plea for help, only to have Luca beat me to the door as he pulls a gun from the back of his waistband. I make it to the bathroom a step behind him to find Toby standing at the bathroom counter, looking at the side of his shirt.

His eyes bug at the sight of us, his focus turning to the gun, his mouth dropping open as if he's about to scream.

"What's wrong?" I push past Luca and place a hand on his arm to encourage him to lower the weapon. "What happened?"

Tobias shrinks into me.

"It's okay." I crouch before him and grab his waist, clinging tight to gain his attention. "Luca thought you were in trouble. He came racing in here to help. Tell me what's wrong."

"There's blood." He twists his shirt to show me the stain on the side of the material. "I think I'm hurt."

My pulse spikes.

I've been hit so many times during the height of an adrenaline rush that I know what it's like not to feel injuries until the intensity wears off.

If he's hurt and I didn't know… If he's dying and I didn't think to check him…

I stand, grabbing his shirt to yank it over his head, then mount a full-scale search of his body, frantically scanning him everywhere. Arms. Stomach. Back. Skull.

I can't find any cuts or marks. There's nothing. Only pure, delicate skin. But I keep searching, making him spin around one more time to triple check.

"I don't think he's injured." Luca approaches, his gun thankfully returned to the back of his jeans. "Even if he was, I'm sure he'd survive. You're a tough kid, aren't you, Tobias? Brave, too."

Toby straightens with the compliment, his tiny muscles moving under my touch. He nods, quick and sharp, the slightest sense of pride ebbing from him.

"Why don't you get him to take a shower or a bath?" Luca asks. "It might help. I can get him a clean T-shirt to wear afterward. Obviously it will swim on him, but it's better than walking around in stained clothes."

More pained beats pummel my chest. I don't like how his kindness affects me. The tiny fingers of comfort latch around my chest, threatening to squeeze me to death. It takes all my strength to ignore my doubt. For Toby's sake.

"What do you say?" I cup his cheek. "Do you think a

relaxing bath will make you feel better? You've been awake for a long time and the water might help you wind down so you can rest for a few hours."

He stares at me with indecision, then shoots a nervous glance at the bulking man blocking the doorway.

"Don't worry, little guy. I'll leave." Luca steps back from the door and awkwardly bumps into the frame as he retreats.

I narrow my gaze, watching as he fumbles then sways on his feet before disappearing from view. Something is wrong with him. *Very* wrong.

"Toby, start getting undressed. I'll be back to run the water in a second." I follow after Luca, my stride long as I catch up to him in the bedroom. "Wait." I grab his arm when he doesn't stop and let go just as fast. My grip on his muscled bicep was a stark reminder of the threat he provides. Of his dangerous abilities.

He turns to look at me, and stumbles. His face is pale, a glimmer of sweat breaking across his brow.

Before I know it I'm latching onto him again, this time trying to keep him upright, the knitted muscle beneath my hands hard and unyielding.

"What's wrong?" I struggle to keep him standing. "Luca?"

He stares straight through me, his forehead creased. "Shit."

"I'll get help." I make for the door only to be stopped by rough hands gripping my upper arms. I freeze, my panic instantaneous.

I brace for violation. All the horrors Luther bestowed upon me lay out like a smorgasbord as I wait for Luca to make his choice.

"I'm fine. I just moved too quick." He releases me and fumbles forward to the bed, allowing me to breathe again.

I don't budge as he slumps onto the mattress, his head hanging, the wisps of his blood-matted hair falling to shroud his eyes.

Bile coats the back of my throat, the nausea coming thick and fast. I didn't realize how much faith I had in him until those hands gripped me tightly. There wasn't trust, but there must've been something else. Something to make me completely blindsided by his aggressive touch.

"I scared you." He massages the uninjured side of his head. "Fuck... I shouldn't have grabbed you."

I remain immobile while I pull myself together.

"Go check on the kid," he mutters. "I'll be out of here in a minute."

I should take his advice. I need distance to think.

It's his pain and the looming threat of losing the only person I may be able to rely on that makes me stay.

"You need to see a doctor," I murmur.

"I'll bounce back in a minute."

I don't believe him. Now I'm paying attention I can see his discomfort increase whenever he moves or speaks. It's only slight, yet always there, following everything he does.

He raises his head, looking up at me through thick lashes. Those eyes are dark, their depth punishing. But it's his dilated pupils that cause me concern.

I suck in a breath. "You've got a concussion."

"Yeah." He shrugs. "I've had worse."

The instinct to take him at his word is strong. I want to have faith in him. And I itch to reject the slight glimmer of trust at the same time.

"If you're not going to see a doctor, you should at least clean your wound."

"No. I'm—"

"A stubborn man who doesn't want to destroy his tough-guy status after surviving a bullet to the skull?"

He huffs out a chuckle. "My tough-guy status is the last thing I'm worried about." He speaks in a lazy drawl, yet the pointedness in his gaze insinuates I'm the focus of his current concern. That I'm all he's worried about. "Besides, I can't get a proper look at the side of my head. I don't even know what I'm up against."

Is he fishing for connection? For trust?

I suck my lower lip between my teeth, staring at him, trying to see the deception I'm sure he must have hidden. Men don't help women. They use. Hurt. Abuse.

Goddammit.

Why can't my life be easy for once? I don't want to keep questioning everything. Everyone. I just want noth-ingness.

No thoughts. No fear. No pain.

No struggle to get my sisters to safety.

"I can take a look. If that's what you want." I shuffle forward, tempting fate, testing this flimsy layer of protec-tion he's shrouded me in. If this is all an act I'd prefer to know now, not later. Not once I've lost myself too far down the torturous path of trust.

He raises his chin, blinking up at me. Silent. Contem-plative.

My heart flutters under his attention, my insides quavering. I'm scared, my fear tightly bottled. It's more than that, too. I tremble for reasons unknown.

The closer I get, the harder it is to think through the

tormented sea swirling inside me. He's a trap. The temptation of his help lays in wait beneath the steel claws of his intentions.

I reach out, my approach tentative.

"Take care of the kid first." He tilts his head away. "He's waiting on you to run the bath."

I'm confused by his rejection, my arm hovering in the space between us, my fingers an inch from his hair.

"Go on. Look after Toby." He pushes from the bed, his hulking frame dwarfing me. "I'll find him a shirt to wear."

I retreat with uncertainty.

At least I understood the threat from Luther. I knew him so well I could anticipate his next move.

Luca is different. I can't foresee anything with him. Not his words or his actions. I can't even understand his claim to want to help me.

I backtrack, turning away from him to walk through the robe, then into the bathroom where Tobias is naked and standing in wait.

I ignore my confusion as I stalk to the bath and turn on the taps, making the water gush like a waterfall.

"Is he a nice man?" Tobias walks to my side. "Because I thought he was, then Dad said he wasn't. Now I don't know what to think because he still seems nice."

I kneel before the bath and swirl the water, buying myself time to answer.

I don't know what to say.

My heart wants to trust the man who protected us with vicious determination. It's my head that reminds me I've fallen victim to the lies of a predator once before.

"He seems genuine." I continue mixing the water. "Don't you think?"

He shrugs and steps into the bath. "I want to like him. But I heard some of the things he said to Dad before he…" There's another shrug, his sorrow building behind those innocent eyes.

I hate that he's hurting. And I detest that a monster's murder is the cause of his pain.

"Sweetheart, I know it's hard to think about your dad being gone. He was your family. But we're going to get through this. I'll make sure of it."

He sits in the building water and pulls his bended legs to his chest. "He hurt you."

I stiffen, unsure how to react. He's never mentioned the reality of my situation before. Not once.

"He hurt you, and Chloe, and the others all the time."

"Yes, he did," I whisper.

"Why?" His brows knit. "Why did he do that?"

Grief hits me. Grief at the life stolen from me, at the years I lost, at the scars I know will never heal, and how this little boy witnessed it all.

"Your father was…" My throat tightens.

"A bad man?" He blinks up at me. "I know he was. But I was scared, and I didn't know how to save you."

I want to sob. To let the tears roam free. If only my body knew how. "It wasn't your job to save me, gorgeous boy. It was a horrible situation and now we need to move on. I'm going to go back to the country I grew up in, and you're going to come with me. We're all going to be all right."

"Nina, Chloe, Abi, and Lilly, too?"

"Yep. All of us."

His lips curve in a smile, the happiness not reaching his

eyes. "I'd like that. I want to get far away from here. Especially from Cole."

"Why Cole?" I reach around him to turn off the taps. "Did he hurt you?"

"No, but he will. He'll punish me for stabbing him. I didn't even do it right. It barely worked, but he was so mad."

"Oh no, sweetheart. I promise he won't hurt you." God, how I hope he won't. "He's a smart man. He knows you didn't want to cause trouble."

The brush of footfalls hits my ears as Luca edges into my periphery. He stands in the doorway, a towel and clothes scrunched in one hand, a bottle of alcohol and a tiny cardboard packet in the other. "Want me to come back later?"

"No. You can actually help set our minds at ease." I push to my feet and attempt to find a relatively clean spot on my blouse to dry the water from my hands. "I was just telling this beautiful boy that Cole wouldn't hold a grudge over what happened between them earlier. Do you agree?"

Luca walks toward us, shrinking the small space with his mountainous frame. "I definitely agree. Cole values family above all else. I'm sure he's just relieved you're safe."

Tobias takes in Luca's words with gradually building trust. "Do you really think so?"

"One hundred percent. You should've heard how excited he was to find out he had a kid brother. I'm sure once things settle down you two will become inseparable."

It's a placation, a kind one, and I can't help turning my back to Tobias to silently mouth, *Thank you.*

Luca inclines his head as he moves to the vanity,

dumping the items in his hands onto the counter. "Toby, is it okay if I stay in here while you bathe? I'm hoping Penny won't mind cleaning me up a little bit."

"I don't mind." Tobias sinks into the bath to lay on his back, the water lapping at his cheeks. "As long as Penny doesn't."

The eyes of an inquisitive stranger stalk me from the reflection in the mirror.

"Are we still good?" he asks.

No, not at all.

Every time I look at him my pulse kicks up a notch. There's so much fear. So much torment.

There's something else, too. Something I refuse to believe is hope.

The mere thought of the weakness inspires anger. I won't let that conniving bitch spread her wings inside my chest.

I have to be tactical. Smart. And if that includes pretending I'm getting close to a stranger, then that's what I'll do.

I suck in a strengthening breath and indicate the counter with a lazy wave of my hand. "Rest back against the vanity and let me take a look at you."

9

______

LUCA

I do as instructed, turning to face her, resting my ass against the vanity counter.

I ignore the hesitation in her voice. I shut down all the bullshit in my head telling me to keep my distance. Like an asshole, I pretend pushing her into trusting me isn't the wrong fucking thing to do.

She walks toward me, her steps hesitant.

"Before you get started—" I cross my feet at the ankles. Laid back. Calm. "—this isn't another attempt to get close so you can attack me, is it?"

"Maybe." She reaches my side and opens the vanity cupboards to my right. "Do you think the third time would be the charm?"

I smirk, appreciating her subtle humor. It's barely there, her expression remaining tight, but the derision is a starting point.

"I noticed you cleaned up the mess I made with that device you were carrying." There hadn't been any sign of the stabby stick I'd stomped into my carpet. "You kept it, didn't you?"

She closes the cupboards and stands tall before me, her silence a blatant answer.

"Does it still work?" I ask.

She holds my gaze, a million thoughts ticking behind those big brown eyes. "I'm not entirely sure."

Her truth is a gift. A fucking brilliant step in the right direction. "You won't need it for long. Once things settle, I can get you whatever weapon you want. I can make sure someone teaches you how to use them, too."

She licks her lower lip, the flick of her tongue fast, almost agitated. If I had to guess, I'd say she doesn't appreciate my attempt to build a bridge between us. My kindness scares her.

"That would be nice." She fobs me off with the half-hearted acknowledgement and moves to my other side. "Can you shuffle over please? I want to check the drawers."

I comply, sliding across the counter. "What are you looking for?"

"A cloth or something to help clean you up."

"You're not going to find anything in there. All the linen is in the hall cupboard." I lean forward, cringe against the pounding protest of my skull, and yank off my shirt. "Use this." I hand over the soiled material. "Douse it in alcohol and it should be fine. I'm going to have to burn it anyway."

She doesn't take the offering. Instead, she retreats a step, her attention riveted on my chest. There's nothing flattering about the way she looks at me. There's only trepidation. Undiluted panic.

Shit.

I didn't contemplate the underlying threat she'd see in my exposed skin. Not that I can think much of anything over the dizzying squeeze of my brain.

"That was a stupid move." I unfurl the crumpled shirt and prepare to pull it back over my head. "I'll go find something else to use."

"No." She reaches out, grasping the material, her fingers brushing mine. "I can do this."

She keeps her gaze averted from mine as she rinses the material in the sink, the pink tinge of blood seeping into the water. She doesn't seem to care about the possible diseases my blood could carry. Then again, she didn't seem to care when Luther was shooting at her either.

She wanted death.

Who knows if she still does?

"I can't imagine how hard it is for you to try and trust me. But there's no threat to you here." I murmur the oath softly, not wanting the kid to overhear our conversation. "We want to protect you. Not hurt you."

She shuts off the taps, wrings the water from my shirt, then lets the sodden weight fall to the sink. She stands there for silent moments, staring at herself in the mirror, her hands clutching the counter.

I want to know what she's thinking. To expose her demons and find a way to slaughter them.

"What's eating away at you?" I grab the wet material, and begin scrubbing my face, my neck, my throat, pretending I'm not ready to hang off her every word.

For a long time she doesn't answer. Instead, she raises her gaze to mine in the mirror, her fragility coming out to play as I feel her guard lower slightly.

"When I was growing up, I always thought horrible people were packaged accordingly." She keeps her voice soft. "I believed bad men were ugly, with easily distinguishable malice. I thought I'd always be able to pick the criminals with horrible intentions because they would look the part. But nothing could be further from the truth. Evil comes with many masks. Some of them more attractive than others."

"I agree." I start rubbing the damp shirt through my hair, the flakes of dried blood dusting the air. "You can't trust a pretty face."

She straightens her shoulders. "Kind words or smooth muscles, either."

She's talking about me. My muscles. My apparent malice.

"That's how Luther took me." She swallows, her tongue snaking out to moisten her lips. "I fell for a kind act and paid the price."

"And now you think I'm doing the same thing?" I keep scrubbing my hair, pretending her continued distrust doesn't get to me.

"I'm not trying to offend you. I just want you to understand my situation. I know you've risked a lot to help me. But until I'm in a place where I feel safe, I'm never going to trust you."

"Then why don't you tell me about this safe place so I can get you there?"

"I wish I could." She holds my gaze, her eyes devoid of hope. "I'm not sure it exists anymore. My nightmare will never be over."

"Of course it will. The memories will fade with time." I

wince and grit my teeth as I hit a sore spot, the added pain ricocheting through my brain.

"Give it here." She holds out a hand for the shirt. "Let me do it."

I oblige, the invigorating boost of victory sliding through my veins. She rinses and wrings the material again, then sidesteps to stand in front of me, making sure to leave a generous amount of space between us. With her arm completely outstretched, she starts to wipe the damp shirt over my jaw, my cheek.

I can't take my eyes off her. Even if I could, I wouldn't want to. She's fucking beautiful. So beautiful I feel like a prick for understanding why someone would want to steal her. "You can come closer."

She doesn't pause her movements. Doesn't even acknowledge I spoke. But after a while she shuffles forward, inch by inch, gaining a better vantage point to clean my wound, her bare toes touching the front of my boots.

She comes close. A breath away. And with each progression the air thickens around us, the atmosphere gaining an edge of trepidation.

It feels like one wrong move will have the peace of this moment transformed into another attempt on my life, or worse, she'll retreat into the defensive, resentful woman who grates on my nerves.

"When I mentioned my nightmare never ending, I wasn't referring to the mental struggle I'm going to be up against. I was talking about Luther's men and how they'll make sure I disappear. They won't stop looking for me."

"They can't look when they're dead."

"And you're going to kill them all?"

"Damn straight."

She pauses, sighs, and shakes her head as she stares longingly over my shoulder. "Believe me, the bad guys always win."

"Well, lucky for you, I haven't been one of the good guys for a while."

She stiffens. Almost imperceptibly. The next dab of the shirt is a direct impact to my bullet wound.

"Fuck me, shorty." I jerk back at the stab of agony. "Can you try keeping the material out of my brain?"

"I-I'm sorry. I didn't mean—"

"Sure you did." I fake a smirk, trying to soften the fear I've reawakened in her. *Jesus.* She's more skittish than a wild animal. "You're trying to destroy my tough-guy status, remember?"

Her lips curve in a barely there smile. It's almost imperceptible. Entirely subtle. The brief glimpse of happiness reaches her eyes, transforming the cornered wild cat into a blindingly brilliant beauty of a woman. But as quickly as the vision hits, the carefree gorgeousness fades.

"You need stitches," she murmurs.

I stare at her, willing the beauty to return. I want to see that smile again. Bigger and brighter. Cemented in place.

My dick pulses with compounding need, the perverted reaction enough for me to right the approaching train wreck.

I clear my throat. "Yeah, I figured as much." I turn my head away to grab the tiny sewing kit I found in the utensils drawer of the kitchen. My idiotic libido is nothing more pain won't fix. "How are you with a needle and thread?"

"I guess that depends on how twitchy you'll be

knowing I'm holding something sharp close to your skull." She takes the kit and opens it up to inspect the contents.

"I've got a pretty thick head. I don't think a sewing needle will penetrate."

Again, I get a brief glimpse of a smile, the curve of her mouth inspiring a more determined pulse from my dick.

Jesus fucking Christ.

Maybe I'm dealing with more than concussion. I must have brain damage. If not, Decker will soon ensure I do.

But not even the thought of being pummeled to a pulp can deter me from being consumed by her. She's mesmerizing. From the swell of her lips, to the gentle sweep of her waist, along with everything in between and surrounding.

She isn't merely beautiful. She's beauty itself.

"I need a chair to get a better vantage point." She raises to the tips of her toes. "I can't see properly from here."

I don't hesitate to kneel before her. I want her to know she's in charge. There's no threat from me.

For long seconds she peers down at me, as if understanding the underlying message in my submission. Her tension eases another notch. Her muscles lose their rigidity.

I win another square in this back and forth board game of ours.

"I'm not the best at this." She pulls a needle and thread from the tiny cardboard packet. "I've had to give stitches a time or two, but I'm not entirely sure what I'm meant to be doing."

"I trust you."

She pauses, the dark depths of her eyes seeming tortured by my admission.

"Just try your best. I can promise you, whatever the result, it will be ten times better than the hack job your brother would give me."

The mention of her brother snaps her out of the contemplation. Her discomfort returns tenfold.

She backtracks to the sink, cleans the sewing needle with the liquor, then returns to pour the liquid over my wound, bringing another slap of pain-induced clarity.

A wet path trails down my neck, my chest, my back. For all I know, I look like an oiled-up stripper on ladies' night. But I remain on my knees, keeping silent as she begins to tentatively stitch my wound.

"Tell me if you need me to stop."

"I'm good." I actually want her to quit being gentle and just slaughter the ever-loving fuck out of my skull. Her delicate fingers are only causing more issues. The soft brush of her touch is enough to make me twitch. "Does Tobias always float like that?"

She nods. "He could lay there for hours. And some days, he does. I think it's his form of meditation."

I lower my voice. "Does he know what happened?"

Her stitching ceases, her fingers paused on my scalp.

"He knows." She leans back to give me a pointed look. "I told him his father's death was an accident. That despite how confident and capable Luther was with a gun, it didn't matter when he stumbled around the edge of the sofa and fell." She shrugs. "He knows his father shot himself with his own gun."

I keep my mouth shut, not wanting to dissolve the cease-fire between us by telling her that story won't hold up for long. Once the shock wears off, the kid is going to realize there were too many gunshots for an accident. It was a fucking battlefield out there.

Then again, maybe that's her plan—to appease Tobias's concerns while he's here, but make him question Cole later.

"*What about Chris?*" I mouth.

Her face hardens. "He knows the truth about Chris, too."

I raise a brow, silently asking what truth she's referring to.

"I told him I killed Chris." She returns to her stitching, tugging the thread harder than necessary, not subtle at all in her request to cut the topic of conversation.

I don't push any further. We've come a long way in the last hour.

I've seen her hope and glimpsed the tiniest bit of her trust.

I won't fuck that up.

"I think I'm done." She leans in, inspecting her handiwork. "I just need to cut the thread."

I bow my head, giving her closer access. "Just use your teeth."

Her breathing hitches. It's only subtle. The barest hint of sound. And I can't help wishing I could hear it in a different context. From pleasure, not fear.

She hesitates long enough for the silence to become awkward. Uncomfortable. I lock every muscle, not wanting the barest twinge to spook her and still she doesn't move.

I'm about to straighten when she lunges toward me, the tension on the string pulled tight before a twang announces she's followed my order.

Her retreat is swift. The slide of her steps moving toward the vanity, the rush of water letting me know she's washing her hands.

I hide a smile from my lips as I drag myself to my feet, making sure to keep my distance as I turn to the mirror. "Thanks."

"You're welcome." She doesn't meet my gaze. Not once as she shuts off the taps and backs away.

Her visual disconnect doesn't stop me from staring at her though. I barely drag my gaze away as I take her place at the sink and cup water in my hands to splash over my face and head.

"You should probably try to keep it dry for a while." She wipes her hands on her stained pants, keeping her attention downcast. "I don't know a lot about infection, but I think moisture doesn't help."

"I'll make sure to do that." I will her to look at me. To trust me. I do it for so long it seems as though a day passes in the thickened silence until footsteps sound in the distance.

"*Luca?*" Cole calls from the bedroom. "Where are you?"

Penny's attention snaps to mine, her eyes flaring before she rushes to the tub.

Fuck.

"The bathroom." I grab the towel stashed beneath the numerous T-shirts I brought in for the kid and lob it at her. "Here. Dry him off with this."

She catches the plush material and spreads it wide as Tobias splashes to his feet.

"Don't panic." She smiles at the boy, the expression fake as she wraps him in the towel. "We're safe, remember?"

Her rigidity doesn't fade as Cole comes to stand in the doorway, Hunt and Decker flanking him from behind.

For a while, nobody speaks. None of them have to. Their visual accusation is loud enough.

The weight of everyone's focus shifts from Penny, to my fucking naked chest, the resulting glower from Decker harsh enough to cut stone.

"I'm told my brother is sick," Cole grates.

Penny lasers a frantic glance my way. Those dark eyes are filled with indecision. She's weighing her options. Wondering if she should trust me or keep forging ahead on her own.

"He isn't sick," I answer for her, holding her gaze. "There's nothing to worry about."

She stares at me, the questioning slowly fading from her features, transforming her look into something more threatening.

The building hardness in her expression is a warning. A blatant you-better-know-what-you're-fucking-doing. And with this, I do. Without a doubt I know she shouldn't fuck with Torian.

"Then why the hell was I told differently?" he asks.

"It was a miscommunication." I wipe the lingering moisture from my face with my forearm. "Tobias is fine."

"Fine?" Torian's eyes narrow. "I was told he was in urgent need of medical attention. Isn't that the story she gave my sister?"

"Like I said, it was a miscommunication." I pin him with a stare. With a silent warning I'm not going to budge. "But it doesn't change the fact her friends are stuck back at your dad's house. We need to get them out before someone is instructed to dispose of evidence."

"They're my family," Penny corrects. "Not just friends. They're my sisters."

"So I've heard." Cole scrutinizes her, the slow appraisal moving from head to toe. He's weighing his options, judging her concern and the worth of her sisters against the risk associated with rescuing them. "Keira is being rather pushy about sending us back to Naxos to get these women. What are your thoughts, Luca?"

Penny's focus snaps to me and in an instant she regresses from strong warrior to begging beauty. I could stand here for hours drowning in her silent pleas, the gentle sweep of her lashes, the subtle waver to her breathing.

"I need more details," I admit. "At the moment, I'm not entirely sure what we're up against, but I don't see why Hunt, Deck, and I can't go on a recovery mission. We could get information while we're there."

"I was thinking the same thing." Torian gives a subtle nod. "I'd be interested in any hard drives you could find. A prisoner would be even better."

"I'm sure that could be arranged." I grab a clean shirt from the counter and slowly drag it over my head, making sure not to bump the newest addition to my scar tally. "If Penny came with us it could save time."

"Fuck off." Decker pushes past Torian to get into the bathroom. "She's not going anywhere."

"Please." Penny ignores her brother and speaks to my boss. "I could get you whatever you want—files, computers, money—I can even show you where the safes are. Nobody else knows that place like I do. Not even the guards have been there as long as I have."

"Me too," the boy adds. "I know all Baba's passwords."

"Over my dead body," Decker snarls. "I won't allow it."

Penny hardens—her face, her posture, those damn eyes. "You're not my keeper." She returns her focus to Torian. "He's a stranger to me. He has no right to make decisions on my behalf."

Decker pulls back as if the verbal attack was physical. We're all quiet as a kaleidoscope of emotions barrage his features. First shock, then pain, and finally volatile fucking fury as he pins me with a glare. "You did this. I don't know how, but you're fucking responsible."

"I didn't do shit." The pound in my head increases, my vision darkening with the onslaught of raised voices. The gift of unconsciousness hovers close, but if I pass out Penny won't get what she wants. Nobody else is going to fight to get her friends back. "I'll make sure she's protected."

Decker snarls. "Like fuck—"

"Stop." Torian raises a hand in warning. "We're moving this conversation into the living room. Let the boy dress in privacy."

He stalks from the doorway.

Nobody follows.

Decker continues to glare at me. Penny remains on edge. And I'm pretty sure Hunt is only hanging around because he enjoys the dramatics.

"You heard him." I push from the vanity, willing my legs to keep holding my weight. "Start moving."

Decker sneers at me before storming from the room, Hunt shadowing.

I wait until their footsteps fade, for everything to dissolve into the distance, and turn to Penny. "You okay?"

She raises a brow. "Are *you*? Your skin has turned grey."

"We're not talking about me right now."

She nudges closer to Tobias and dries his hair with the corner of the towel. "I've been through worse than an argument with my brother."

That goes without saying. The thought of what she endured at the hands of Luther sits like a lead weight in my gut.

"I can look after myself." She keeps ruffling the kid's hair with the towel. "I just need you to convince them to take me when you go back to Naxos."

"I'll try." I'm not sure I want to make promises. I'm not even sure earning her trust is the right thing to do. "Why don't you freshen up while you're in here? I couldn't find any pants to fit you, but I brought in an extra shirt. And there's a lock on the door, if that helps."

I don't wait for a reply before leaving the enclosed space, my steps wonky as I enter the bedroom to come face-to-face with barely contained fury.

"I don't know what the fuck you've done to turn her against me," Decker seethes quietly, "but I swear on my life, you're going to pay."

"She's in shock. Give her space to sort herself out."

"And what about you? Are you giving her space? Because it doesn't fucking look like it. Seems to me, with that fucking stripper show, that you're trying to take advantage of her."

"I'm trying to show her I'm not a threat. She needs—"

"What she needs is her fucking family," he cuts me off. "Her *real* family. And you're building a wall between us."

My temples pound harder with his raised voice. "Look,

Deck, earlier she was trying to stab me with a fucking sedative-filled syringe and refused to admit she even had a brother. Now she's willing to at least acknowledge you, and isn't trying to lay me on my ass. It's all forward momentum. So ease up and stop acting like another piece of shit who wants to control her."

His eyes flare. "I'm not trying to control her, you self-righteous son of a bitch. I'm trying to help her."

"So am I. I think it's clear whose tactics are working better."

He chuckles, the sound harsh. "You're getting on my last nerve, motherfucker. I suggest you back off."

For anyone else, I probably would. I'd bow out, giving this pounding head of mine a breather from the bullshit. "I can't. Not when it comes to her."

His upper lip curls, exposing teeth. "So seduction is the game, is it? Your kink is damsels in distress."

I scoff and start for the hall. "I'm done with this."

"Fuckin' answer me." He rushes to block my path and shoves at my chest.

The resulting squeeze of my migraine is enough to make vomit clog the back of my throat. I breathe through the need to hurl and clench my fists. "Did she look like a fucking damsel to you?"

"She looks fucking broken." His nostrils flare, his chest rising and falling with heavy breaths. "She looks like a skeleton of the sister I used to know, and here you are pushing her back into hell."

"Get out of my way. I don't have the patience for your shit right now."

"*My* shit? *My fucking shit?*" He cracks his knuckles. "Then let me put you out of your misery."

The thought of him knocking me senseless is more comforting than it should be. Unconsciousness would be a blessing. Unfortunately, it's not an option. "You're going to hit a guy with a concussion?"

"No, I'm going to hit a guy who's pitching a fucking tent for my sister."

"Yeah." I nod, despite the resulting pound from the movement. "That's exactly what I'm doing. I was pitching a tent when I shoved her out of the line of fire and took a bullet to the head. And I sure as shit was pitching when I tackled her to the ground when Luther was trying to shoot her in the back. So many tents were pitched I could house a fuckin' army."

"You think sarcasm is going to get you out of this?" He steps closer. Right in my face. "I can see what you're up to."

"Then start swinging. One punch and I'll be out like a light."

"Perfect." He cocks a fist.

"For you maybe. But not for your sister and her friends. As it is, there's only three of us to take on however many assholes guard Luther's house." I throw my arms wide. "But it's your choice. Do you want instant gratification or do you actually want to help her?"

He jabs a finger at my chest. "Don't ever fucking question that I want what's best for her."

"I'm not questioning that. I'm saying you're letting your emotions get the better of you. She's fucking scared. I swear she doesn't know what she's doing apart from acting on instinct. And at the moment, the hope that comes with seeing you is obviously too much to take."

He pauses, blinking slowly as his wrinkled forehead loses some of the tension.

"Stop thinking about what *you* want and what *you* need, and let her run this show," I mutter. "Doesn't she deserve that much?"

His jaw continues to tick, but eventually he takes a step back, raking a hand through his hair. "I want to help her. I can't fucking stand being kept at arm's length after thinking I'd lost her."

"I get it. Anyone in their right mind would've expected your reunion to go down a lot fucking happier than this. But it didn't and there's nothing you can do about it. Give her space. And time. She'll come around. *Then* you can beat the shit out of me." I shrug. "Or at least you can try."

He gives a breathy chuckle, the sound vicious. "Yeah. I guess you're right. Delayed gratification will do just fine." He shoves me again, the whiplash jolting my head and blinding me for an instant.

I close my eyes as his heavy steps leave the room, the sound barely heard over the ringing in my ears. I'm in deep shit here. Any minute now and I could keel over, no punch necessary.

Fuck.

I sway with the building weight bearing down on me. I mentally battle to remain conscious.

"I'm sorry he's taking this out on you." Penny's whispered voice acts as a balm to my pain and a fucking trigger all at once.

I open my eyes. She stands in the doorway to the bathroom, Tobias at her side.

"I don't blame him." I squeeze the bridge of my nose

and start for the hall. "You should get some rest while you can."

I don't pause for a reply, I stalk my ass out of there and into the living room, finding Keira, Hunt, Decker, and Torian seated around the dining table.

"Where's Sarah?" I drag out a chair opposite Penny's brother to keep an eye on the aggressive motherfucker.

"Escorting Anissa home." Torian drinks from a steaming mug. "They should be halfway to the jet by now."

"We're stranded? Again?" Jesus fucking Christ. We got into this mess because these assholes called our jet back to Portland. Now, we're stuck all over again. "Is that a good idea?"

"Another aircraft is on standby," he growls, making it obvious he doesn't appreciate my questioning. "We can fly out of here at a moment's notice. Now, tell us what's going on with her. What's she playing at?"

"She's not playing at anything. Her actions could be long-term PTSD. Or shock from today. Who the fuck knows? Only time will tell."

"Time isn't something we have a lot of. Especially not if you're suggesting taking her back to Naxos."

"Can we drop that line of thought right now?" Decker mutters. "She's not going back there."

"Protest all you like, but she's our greatest asset in helping to retrieve the other women, along with whatever information we can get our hands on. God knows the shit Luther was up to. This might be our only chance to find out."

Long moments of tension-filled silence pass. Nobody talks. Nobody moves. We all sit there, weighing our options or lack thereof. It's a case of saving the other women or letting them die, which, to me, means there's no option at all.

"Do you really think it's necessary to take her?" Keira asks. "Can't she just tell you everything she knows?"

"No, I think he's right." Torian leans back in his chair. "We've been to Luther's house once already. And I can't think how we'd get past the guarded gate without her. Those rifle-toting assholes won't let us in without permission. She could be our ticket inside."

"Fucking hell." Decker wipes a hand down his face. "There's gotta be another way."

"There might be. The question is—do we have enough time to figure it out?" I return to massaging my temples. Then the back of my neck. I do everything and anything to try and relieve the pressure in my skull. "Penny has already said Luther's men will start taking action if their boss doesn't make contact within a certain amount of time."

"How long is that?" Hunt asks.

"She doesn't know." I close my eyes, the lack of bright light helping to ease the pain in my head. "Our window for action might have already passed."

I relax into the darkness, my nausea receding. All I need is a few more minutes to pull my shit back together.

"What if it's a trap? She doesn't seem all that keen on sharing our company," Hunter adds. Maybe she wants to go back to the place where she feels comfortable. This could be a case of 'better the devil she knows.'"

"It's not."

My pulse spikes at the sound of her voice and I force myself not to react. I don't raise my head. I don't open my eyes either, not until Decker whispers a harsh curse under his breath.

I push upright and see her walking toward us dressed in one of the spare T-shirts I'd left in the bathroom. And no fucking pants.

The sight of her is pure fragility.

A gorgeous figure dwarfed by baggy material.

It's the strong set of her shoulders, the confident stride, and the high arc of her neck that make it clear she's not letting her guard down anytime soon.

"I don't want to go back to Naxos for any reason other than to get my sisters." She wraps her arms around her middle, the loose material hitching higher to reveal more of her perfect thighs. "And I promise I'm not setting a trap. As far as I know, nobody else was aware of Luther's motives for coming out here. His guards won't suspect foul play. At least not yet."

"How do you know?" Hunter grates. "I understand you've been stuck with him for a while, but you can't tell me you were by his side every minute of the day."

"Hunter," Keira warns. "Tread lightly."

"I am. I just can't comprehend the son of a bitch divulging information in front of one of his..." The sentence hangs and tense silence is the only thing left to fill the void.

"One of his sex slaves?" Penny finishes for him. "You can say it. A few words aren't going to break me."

Everyone winces, except me.

I see her strength. The determination. It's beyond admirable.

"And you're right," she continues. "He held his cards close to his chest. I rarely heard his plans for anything, except for the week when he punished me like a dog. I was leashed and dragged along by his side. He never let me out of his sight. I overheard every conversation he had for seven days. And none of them involved him sharing information with anyone other than Chris, Robert, and a few other people who I've never met before. His guards were always kept on a need-to-know basis."

Anger consumes me, the heat of rage inspiring a tick to form at the top of my right cheek.

Luther treated her like a dog. A fucking animal. And I can see from the ease with which she talks about it that it was far from her worst punishment.

I push from the table, breaking the silence and stealing the pity-filled glances away from Penny as I go in search of caffeine. "We can make a surprise attack."

"Maybe some of you could." Her gaze follows me. "That's still an option. But it's better to approach legitimately. Distract the guards with our arrival. We can pretend Luther wanted me taken back without him. That way any covert action is less likely to be noticed. It also gets a car inside the gates so we've got an easier escape."

"It also makes whoever is in that car a sitting duck," Hunt drawls. "It's too risky."

"No riskier than someone scaling the wall and getting stuck on the inside." She holds my gaze as if I'm the person she needs to convince. "They're trigger-happy. One glimpse of action and they'll shoot. They won't pause to ask questions."

"And neither will I." Decker shoves from the table, his chair scraping along the tile. "I also can't sit here and participate in planning something that will risk your life all over again. I'll help with whatever needs to be done, but I refuse to encourage any of this shit."

He stalks for the hall, Keira scooting from her chair to quickly follow after him.

Penny doesn't watch him leave. She keeps her gaze on me, her silent regret passing between us. I see her—the fragility beneath the strength, the love for her brother hidden behind her shields.

"Don't worry. He'll be fine." I pivot to the cupboards and pull out a tin filled with cookies. "You still haven't eaten."

"I'm not hungry."

"You're either lying, which I've already warned you about, or you're still in shock. And both would improve with a sugar fix." I place the tin on the counter, remove the lid. "It's non-negotiable, Penny." I slide the tin toward her, then do the same with a plate. "I need to be able to rely on you if we're taking you back to Naxos. That means a full stomach and maybe some caffeine, too."

She glances at Hunter and Torian, who have already returned to a conversation filled with strategy and weapons tactics.

"Don't worry about them." I tap the side of the tin. "Keep your eyes on the prize."

Her gaze softens, the tension slightly leaving her frame. "Thank you."

The appreciation is barely audible. It sinks into me though. Soul-deep.

"Don't mention it." I rifle through the drawers as she grabs something to eat, and pull out a pad and pen to place down beside her. "Once you're done I'm going to need you to sketch a map of what we're up against."

"I can do that." She holds a hand over her mouth as she chews. "I can also mark where the safes are and their pin codes."

"Perfect."

She keeps eating, leaving that delicate hand covering her lips. "But in return I need you to do one more thing for me."

And there it is—the foreboding, the ten steps back to my slight forward momentum. I can already tell I won't like her request. I'll hate it and want to comply in equal measure. "And what's that, shorty?"

"I need you to give me a gun."

10

PENNY

Luca didn't give me a gun. He did, however, laugh in an understated, totally endearing and equally demeaning way before declining my request with a subtle apology.

"You're too volatile at the moment," he'd said. "And it will ruin this tough-guy thing I've got going if a woman under my protection starts fighting her own battles."

He'd meant the latter as a joke.

I didn't find it funny.

But he, along with Hunter and Torian, listened in silence as I talked them through my rough sketch of the house and yard. I told them where I thought the guards might be—inside and out—and gave them my knowledge of the weapons they should be holding—a rifle and knife —along with my assumption of any training they may have had—limited to none.

I was treated like an integral part of the team. They asked innumerable questions, ran through strategies, and made me eat to increase my energy levels while we came up with different plans of action, each option having multiple contingencies.

By the time they were ready to make a move, night had fallen, and Tobias had claimed a few hours of awake time to become marginally settled in Keira's presence.

She was good with him. Too good. Which pissed me off. His naive kiddo brain took in every kind word she said like a sponge. He gobbled up her kindness and generosity as if it were edible gold. So now I like her even less.

Their incremental bond wasn't enough to make me feel comfortable leaving him on the island, but their connection appeased me to the point where I could step onto the boat knowing he was safer with Keira than he'd be back at home.

Then there's my brother, the man who no longer tries to meet my gaze. The one whose aura seeps with such deep sorrow as we race over the moonlit water I can't stop my breath from catching whenever I look his way.

"Are you warm enough?" Luca settles next to me on the boat's bench seat, his attention on the goosebumps along my arms.

"I'm good." The sea breeze makes my loose shirt billow at the hem, the sweep of mother nature's kiss the only comforting sensation out here in solitude. It's the beauty before the approaching storm, but I refuse to let the thought of what's to come send me into a spiral.

I need to stop thinking about the possibility of the guards not acting according to how I anticipate. Or that my sisters could already be dead. The unknowns try to haunt me like a conniving devil on my shoulder. I can't give in to the darkness. Not yet.

"You nervous?" Luca's voice is barely audible over the rush of water against the hull.

He makes me nervous.

Returning to the only home I've known for the last eighteen-plus months seems more natural in comparison. At least I can predict what will happen inside those walls. The suffocating fear of what comes next is almost a comfort because of its familiarity. It's what I'm used to. What I know.

With Luca, I'm in unchartered territory.

"I'm cautious," I admit. "I don't hold the same confidence you all have."

"You're our main priority. We're not going to let anything happen to you."

His protection attempts to seep into me, the wisps of kindness brushing over my extremities. I'd love for the effects to sink deeper. To penetrate. If only my self-preservation didn't see his ability to soften me as a threat.

"You all seem to know exactly what you're doing," I murmur. "How can you have confidence when you're going into a situation where you know you'll be outnumbered more than two to one?"

He grips the bench seat on either side of his thighs and ponders his answer for longer than necessary. He opens his mouth, only to close it, then glances away.

"You're faking the confidence, aren't you?" I try to read him. To see what he's attempting to hide. "This is all a huge risk."

"Of course it's a risk. Doesn't mean I'm not confident. I know what I'm doing."

"How? This situation can't be a common occurrence."

He pauses, his gaze gentle. "I've had training."

"Training? How can you train for—"

"I was a SEAL, Penny."

I pull back an inch, my surprise hitting me hard as he glances away. He seems embarrassed by his honorable past.

"I don't understand." I lean to the side, reclaiming his gaze. "Why did you—"

"It's not up for discussion."

Right… his past is a touchy subject. I guess I should be pleased we have something in common, but what he tries to hide only leaves me more unsettled.

"What about the others? I doubt my brother became a SEAL while I was here. What training does he have? Does he have experience with this type of thing? Is he used to killing people, too?"

His expression remains impassive, neither confirming nor denying. "What Decker does and doesn't have experience with is something you should discuss with him. I'm not getting between the two of you again."

My pulse increases as I picture Sebastian as a murderer. I see visions of him killing people. Fighting for his life. Gunning down strangers. The aggression doesn't fit what I know of the man from my past. It doesn't mesh at all.

"I want to know if he's going to be able to look after himself." The question grazes my throat, the hint of a plea layered in my tone. "He's different from the man I grew up with. He's a stranger now."

"Then get to know him." He jerks his chin at Sebastian, standing beside Hunter at the steering wheel. "I'm sure he'd appreciate you attempting to talk to him." He pushes to his feet, distancing me from necessary answers.

"Please." I reach out to stop his escape, my fingers an

inch from contact before I retract at the last second. "Just tell me if he's capable of going through with this. Is he able to kill someone in cold blood?"

He glances down at my hand as my arm retreats, then slowly raises his gaze to mine. "He's capable."

Another part of me dies.

After everything I've been through, I wouldn't have thought it possible. But there it goes, the sinking feeling in my stomach expanding to take over my chest.

Despite our plan already being in motion, a part of me had hoped for Luca's uncertainty. That he didn't know if Sebastian was one of *them*. The bad guys. The brutal.

Not only did his words confirm it, his pity-filled gaze cements the walls of the hollowness carved out inside me.

Sebastian isn't Sebastian anymore.

"Hunter is more than capable, too," Luca adds. "So you've got nothing to worry about."

I scoff out a derisive laugh, hoping the effort will dislodge my vulnerability. "I wasn't overly concerned about him. The vibe he gives off is threatening enough."

A grin tweaks Luca's lips, the sly expression slightly endearing in the glow of the moon. "He may look scary, but he's got a soft side. If his woman asked him to put on a dress and perform a ballet recital, I'm pretty sure he'd comply without skipping a beat."

I raise my brows, not buying his bullshit. Not caring enough to voice it either. I'm already in mourning for my brother. I can't believe the gentle protector is gone. That he's now working for the enemy.

"You'll understand once you meet Sarah." Luca continues. "She's not the kind of woman you deny."

"Pretty?" I assume.

"Deadly." His humor fades. "Don't get me wrong—she's attractive, but she's the type of woman who could slit a throat with a smile on her face. It's like catnip to the big guy."

I bristle at the mental image of this woman. Lethal beauty. Black heart.

I'm out of my depth here. Surrounded by psychopaths. Then there's Luca, with his harsh promises and penetrating stare. Why does everyone else scare me, yet he's become some strange source of stability?

"You've got nothing to worry about, shorty." He takes a step back, preparing to walk away. "I'm not going to let anything happen to you."

And then there's that nickname. *Shorty.* The one word which is far preferable to the things I've been called during the last years. There's the slightest hint of an endearment to it. A lingering compliment of sorts.

But I'm not short. In comparison to him, maybe. Far from it, in relation to other women.

It's just one of the many thoughts plaguing me as I'm left alone for the rest of the ride into the Naxos port.

Even once we arrive, Hunter and Sebastian disembark without a glance in my direction. They know the drill as they each carry a duffel onto the pier, the bags stocked with guns, ammo, and communication devices.

It's Luca who attempts to help me from the boat, his arm outstretched, waiting for me to take his offering.

"I can't." I keep my expression blank in case anyone in the distance is paying us attention. "You're not allowed to touch me."

"Shit." He quits the gentlemanly gesture with a wince.

I don't think it's from the mistake though. It's his head. "You're still in pain."

"The bumpy ride wasn't exactly my best friend. But I'll be fine once we're on land." He glances around the quiet port. "Is there anything else I need to be reminded of?"

I don't answer. I'm too busy studying him—the wrinkles of pain, the skin tone lacking a healthy glow.

"Penny?" He raises a brow of impatience.

"I'm to be treated like Luther's girlfriend in public. Not a slave." I wave a hand to indicate my lack of clothing. "Like we discussed, you need to act like we've been out swimming all day. The police don't appreciate tourists nagging them to check on my welfare. So act normal. No degradation or punishments."

"Jesus Christ," he mutters. "I wasn't going to—"

"I'm just letting you know you're to act professional while I'm in the open. It's in front of Luther's guards or contacts where you'll need to treat me differently."

His jaw tightens. "I won't be treating you like shit regardless of our company."

"You will if you don't want to cause suspicion."

His lip curls, the faintest rumble emanating from his throat.

"What the fuck are you two doing?" Hunter yells from the pier. "Hurry up."

I keep my attention on Luca. On the beautiful intricacies of the disgust written all over his face. He feels sorry for me and I both appreciate and despise his reaction. He doesn't even know the half of what I've been through and yet he harbors pity.

"We're coming." I climb from the boat and wait for Luca to reach my side before we head toward land.

The march forward is accompanied by coded murmurs between the men surrounding me.

"Two at three o'clock," Sebastian says.

"One at ten," from Hunter.

"Three on the balcony at four," comes from the lethal man at my side.

Their constant chatter drills into my head, increasing my unease. I'm used to being surrounded by arrogant confidence, my captors well aware the only eyes daring to look at them would be from curious tourists or enviable deviants.

Now, everything is different.

I'm flanked by a protector. My safety is a priority. Yet I feel more vulnerable than ever. The slightest possibility of freedom has given me something to lose.

Everything to lose.

"So, in public you're treated like a girlfriend?" Luca shoots me a glance, his gaze falling to my feet. "But you weren't given shoes."

"We're on an island. A lack of shoes isn't out of the ordinary."

"How 'bout a lack of pants?" Hunter interrupts. "I don't know one hot-blooded guy who wouldn't pay you attention."

"Suspicion and attention are two different things. One requires police intervention, the other would increase Luther's ego. So, no, my lack of clothing isn't an issue. If anything, it's more acceptable than the full-length pants I wore out of here earlier."

"For the love of..." Sebastian runs a hand through his hair. "I wish I was the one to kill that motherfucker. He had all his bases covered, didn't he?"

They have no idea. I don't want them to either.

The more they learn, the deeper my shame will sink. I don't want them aware of the things I've done. The person I've become.

We reach land and walk through the parking lot to the street, the stabbing asphalt against the soles of my feet a welcome distraction as we approach a man standing beside a compact car, another vehicle parked directly behind it.

"You Luca?" the guy asks, his Greek accent heavy.

"Yeah. Are these our cars?" Luca doesn't leave my side, remaining mere inches away as the man lobs two sets of keys his way.

"Yes. Park them back here when you're done and drop the keys into the locked box over there." He points to a mailbox-type metal locker a few feet along the footpath, then returns his attention to our group. Specifically me, a grin appearing the longer his eyes linger. "I hope you enjoy your stay in Naxos."

He's recognized me. Who I am. *What* I am.

How could he not when I've been branded for years?

"She's a sexy little thing, isn't she?" Luca treats me exactly how he vowed not to moments earlier. "Feisty, too."

His descent into slimy arrogance is so flawless I shiver. The cocky tilt to his lips doesn't help.

"Luther's pretty Penny," the stranger drawls. "She's the stuff of folklore. Men around here would sell their wives just for a taste."

"Luther's not here," I grate through a fake smile. "Why not take the opportunity to indulge in your fantasies?"

The guy laughs. "There's that spite I've heard so much about. You trying to lure me to my death, whore?"

Whore.

The description shouldn't faze me after the years of repetition. I should be immune. Yet the degradation coats me in a layer of grime thicker than anything I've experienced now that I'm in the presence of saviors instead of monsters.

"One can only hope," I snarl.

The man continues to chuckle. "Maybe I will." He steps closer, his eyes raking a trail over my billowing T-shirt. "Maybe I'll teach you to keep that smart mouth closed."

"Please do." Luca steps closer to me. "Everyone keeps making it clear that I can't put hands on her, but they never said anything about scrawny assholes who don't know their place."

Again, he says it so smoothly. With calm and poise and a shocking amount of level-headed arrogance. And again, I shudder, this time in pleasure.

The man doesn't quit his laughter as he beams a bright smile. "I'm only playing." He backtracks, moving from the sidewalk to the desolate street. "I will leave you to enjoy your night."

He continues to a nearby car, his taunting gaze still on mine as he climbs inside and drives away.

All the while, my protectors remain quiet around me, the silence growing thick.

Sebastian scrubs a hand over his face, probably trying to wipe away the shame I've placed upon our family. Hunter is tense, his clenched fist clutching the duffel at his side. Then there's Luca, the man whose fierce attention burns the side of my face. He's staring at me. Judging me.

He's seeing all the things I've done in an effort to keep air in my lungs. He's picturing the depravity. The sickening reality.

"He'll be dead by the end of the week," he murmurs. "I swear it on my life."

His vow catches me off guard. I thought I'd receive a reprimand for my spite. Or a warning not to draw additional attention. Instead, he gifts me with the promise of murder.

"Let's get the fuck out of here." Hunter dumps his duffel on the sidewalk, opens the zipper and pulls out the communication devices stashed inside, passing one to Luca and another to Sebastian. "Put them on in the car. We've got too many eyes on us here."

He refastens the bag and stands, handing over the heavy weight to my brother. "We'll give you a ten-minute head start. Let us know if you need more time."

Sebastian nods, then turns to me, a duffel weighed at each of his thighs, his gaze solemn. I don't want to read into his silence. I can already hear his thoughts.

He wants to say goodbye. Maybe even good luck.

I glance away, my nose tingling at the thought of the danger he's about to place himself in. The danger *I'm* placing him in because I refuse to leave this nightmare without my sisters.

"Look after her." He lugs the duffels to the closest car to place them on the passenger seat. "I'm holding you both responsible." He slams the door shut, then rounds the hood, not saying another word before he slumps into the vehicle and takes off.

I squeeze my eyes shut, unable to watch him drive away.

Ten minutes is going to be the only thing separating us. Six hundred measly seconds, while each heartbeat creates a cavern of space between us. Despite who he's become, I couldn't live with the thought of being the cause of his death.

My eyes burn behind the closed lids. I have enough guilt to contend with. I can't withstand anymore.

"He's going to be okay," Luca whispers. "This will all be over soon."

I hope so. I don't know how much more of this adrenaline high I can take. The arrhythmia won't stop. The tremble in my hands is incessant. And the pessimistic thoughts continue to multiply.

"Picture the end result." His gravel-rich voice brushes my ear. "Focus on what it's going to be like once we're out of here. If not, your thoughts can become your biggest enemy."

I comply, squeezing my eyes tighter until I see the smiling faces of my sisters as I help lead them to safety. I can't wait to tell them they're free. Or to fully drown in the sensation myself.

I'll apologize to Chloe and make sure she knows I'm sorry for remaining silent while Luther made her a guinea pig to the sedative trial. And I'll beg her forgiveness for whatever the guards took liberties to do to her limp body after Tobias and I were escorted from the mansion.

I keep picturing those moments as footsteps sound a few feet away, followed by a car door opening and closing.

"Come on." Rough fingers provide a feather of friction against my arm, the touch lasting the slightest second before withdrawing. "We need to get moving."

I blink him into focus, his comforting concern bearing

down on me. There's something in those hazel eyes that undo me. They unravel my focus. Create havoc. I'm sure he knows, too, because he's the first to look away and start toward the remaining car.

"You're in the back," he offers over his shoulder as he makes his way to the driver's side and climbs in behind the wheel.

Hunter already rides shotgun.

I'm left on my own. Out in the open. With no cage or threatening figure by my side. It's a strange sensation. Welcoming and suffocating at the same time. I can breathe freely, the air seeming to carry twice as much oxygen.

Hunter lowers his window, his narrowed focus silently telling me to hurry up.

I'm not ready. Not yet. Just one more moment. One more breath before commonsense has to take over and I need to pretend I'm still a prisoner.

"I'm not an athlete," he mutters, "so run if you like. I'm not going to chase you. But if you want to help your friends I'm fucking ready to bust some skulls."

"I'm not running." I stalk to the car and slide in behind him. "I want those busted skulls more than you do."

"Then let's do this." Luca starts the ignition and drives lazily through the narrow streets, taking wrong turns and doubling back more than once on his way to Luther's house.

I lean forward as my panic ratchets up a notch. "Do you know where you're going?"

"It's all in the plan." He takes another wrong turn. "We're still buying Decker time to get set up, and I want to make sure we don't have a tail."

"Oh." I settle back into my seat, slightly appeased.

The confidence in Luther's men had always been something I despised. And somehow, the trait on a good guy has the opposite effect.

No, not a good guy. Just a different type of bad. I can't forget that.

"I'm headed in the right direction now, though, right?" He flicks me a glance in the rear-view. "Straight down this road, then take the next two lefts?"

I nod. "Yeah."

The closer we get, the more my pulse builds. My nausea increases at the thought of my sisters already being dead. Slaughtered. I've seen too much death already. Vacant eyes and lifeless bodies. Sisters who came and went from this world, the scars of their suffering the only thing left behind.

"You okay?" Luca asks. "What's wrong?"

My throat tightens, the bile climbing from my stomach. I can't escape the darkest depths of my memories. I'm battered with snapshots. Pummeled with remembered sounds. I know what those guards are capable of and if they've found out Luther was murdered—

"Penny?" Luca reaches into the back seat to jostle my leg. "What's going on?"

"Nothing." I fight the panic and swallow down the sickening taste building at the back of my throat. "I'm fine."

"Fine." Hunter scoffs. "Fuck I hate when women say that."

"It's not too late to back out." Luca returns both hands to the steering wheel, his scrutiny heavy from the rear-view mirror. "All you need to do is say the word."

"I'm ready." I force conviction into my tone. "And

we're almost there, so quit worrying about me and focus. One wrong move and we're all dead."

Hunter chuckles. "That's one seriously messed up pep talk. I like your style."

The car slows as we reach the corner to Luther's street and Luca raises a finger to his ear, repositioning his comm piece. "Decker is ready. We're good to go."

I know what that means. My brother is already up there. At the house. Preparing to kill… or be killed.

"Is he okay?" I lean forward again. "Did he say anything else?"

"If there was something wrong we would've heard." Luca continues to stalk me from the mirror. "You need to relax. Sit back. Breathe."

"I'm breathing," I murmur.

He grins, the brightness entering his eyes a soothing blanket over my frazzled nerves. I don't know how he does it. He's harsh yet gentle. Domineering, aggressive, threatening, and so entirely reassuring at the same time.

It's unnatural.

No doubt an effect of my growing instability.

The car picks up speed as we round the bend and drive at a normal pace to Luther's property. The extravagant metal gates gleam in the moonlight, the door to my cage waiting for me to slip back where I belong.

"Game faces, people." Hunter's voice is barely audible. "It's time to dish out some karma."

I do as planned, sit tall, scowl in place, hands in my lap. I look straight ahead, not focusing any of my concern on the guard who approaches from the darkness, his rifle aimed at the car as Luca lowers his window.

This is it—the moment where any or all of us could be

slaughtered because I made an incorrect assumption about the guards' knowledge.

"Hey, buddy," Luca greets. "How's things?"

"Back away." The middle-aged guy snarls, his accent heavy, the barrel of his weapon dropping to pin Luca in the chest. "This is private property."

"I know. I was here yesterday, remember?"

There's a pause, each beat of silence growing thicker.

"With Cole," he adds. "Luther's son."

I wait, hoping for the first sign of our success, when our failure will easily be announced with a gunshot. But there's no reaction. Not in understanding or threat. If the guard has any inkling Luther left here to attack Cole and Luca this gun-toting asshole isn't showing it.

"You shouldn't be here unannounced." He repositions the rifle at his hip. "What do you want?"

I let out a long breath and swallow to alleviate the desert in my mouth. The guard's question is the first sign of our possible success. He has no idea we're a threat. And yet the progress only adds more pressure to my insides.

"Luther requested some private family time with his boys. So he sent us here to enjoy ourselves. You know—" Luca gives a cocky chuckle. "—With the women."

The weight increases, the discomfort squeezing my stomach, shoulders, neck. I ignore how easily Luca plays his role, not wanting to drown in my thoughts of how he can keep effortlessly switching from protector to predator.

"No. I know nothing of this." The guard jabs his rifle toward the car. "Leave."

"Leave?" Hunt leans forward to meet the guy's line of sight. "Even when we've got one of Luther's girls with us?" He jerks a thumb toward me. "I'm pretty sure he'll be pissed if we sate our boredom with this one."

The guard leans down, his dark features peering into the window opposite mine, his narrowed eyes raising goosebumps on my skin. "Why is she with you?"

"We just fucking told you. Luther asked us to bring her back. He said he wanted uninterrupted family time and when the big guy gives an order, you obey, right?" Luca reaches into his jacket and pulls out a gun, pinching it between two fingers so it dangles without threat. "And he reminded us of the no-weapon rule, too." He hangs the pistol out the window. "If you don't believe me, call him. Just be aware he's going to be fuckin' pissed at the interruption."

The guard's attention flicks between me, the gun, then Luca, and back again. He's weighing up the bluff. "*Léne tin alítheia?*" He speaks my way, his question asking about my chauffeur's honesty.

"*Fysiká,*" I sneer. "Why else would I be here?"

His lip curls, his hatred unhidden as he steps forward and snatches the gun before jamming it into the waistband of his pants. "Give me your gun, too." He lowers the barrel of his rifle while he speaks to Hunter. "If you're caught with a weapon inside those walls you will be shot without warning."

Hunter complies, reaching across Luca to hand over his pistol.

We're being allowed inside.

The guard is letting Luca and Hunter fulfil their perversions, which means my sisters are still alive. No alarms have been sounded. The best-case scenario has been laid at our feet.

My heart pumps faster. Anticipation has my fingers twitching in my lap.

"*Échoume episképtes,*" the guard grates into the communication device stashed into the sleeve of his suit jacket. "Luther's orders. Give them access to the *gynaíkes.*" He returns his focus to the men in the front seat. "No more guns?"

"No more guns," Hunter answers. "Just the big pistol I'm packin' for the ladies."

I close my eyes, despising his casual reference to rape.

"Enjoy yourself."

That's the last I hear of the guard as the gates whir apart, allowing us entry.

I know what comes next. This part of the plan was set in stone. It's the only reason I open my eyes to seek out the guard returning to his position in the shadows.

"Look away, Penny," Luca demands.

I won't.

I pin my glare on the guard, his mimicked expression holding mine as a darkened figure creeps up behind him.

Our car moves forward, the sound of the engine and the opening gates enough to mask my brother's approach, but I stare harder at the guard, glare with more ferocity, hoping somehow to distract Satan's henchman from the sentence that approaches.

"Penny," Luca warns. "Look away."

My heart stops the moment Sebastian grabs the guard around the neck, pulling him backward and off-balance. There's a sheer second of surprised panic. A slash of a glinting knife. A brief struggle. Then death.

My brother kills the man right before me and yet it's done so easily, so effortlessly, it seems like fiction. A movie. There was no pause for contemplation or compassion.

"For fuck's sake, Penny, I told you to look the other way."

"Let her watch." Hunter comes to my defense. "I'm sure she's seen worse."

"Just because she's seen it before doesn't mean she has to see it now." Luca presses his foot harder on the accelerator. "And besides, she needs to fucking listen if we're going to get out of here alive."

"I'll listen." I continue to watch my brother as he drags the lifeless body toward a head-high bush. "But only when your instructions involve getting my friends to safety. Don't pretend you know what's best for me."

He growls, his anger a low vibration as we pass the gates. I chance a glance through the back window, trying to gain another glimpse of Sebastian.

"Eyes to the front," Luca commands. "Keep playing your role."

This time I obey, slumping into the seat as the car curves around the long drive to pull up in front of the overbearing mansion. I try not to let foreboding consume me, but that house has a soul. A dark one. It beckons to me, whispering promises of torture.

"Deck just took down another target." Hunter presses a hand to his hidden earpiece. "He seems to think these guys are easy prey."

I unfasten my belt to scoot forward. "Tell him not to become complacent. Some of them are brutal."

"Hear that, Deck? Your sister said not to get cocky." Hunter glances over his shoulder at me. "Would you normally be eager to get up close and personal like that? Or should you be keeping your distance?"

I can't help it. I'm anxious. Completely and utterly unsettled.

The engine is cut as I slide back. Seatbelts are unfastened. The men climb outside. Then Luca is at my door, pulling it wide to wait for me to join them.

I don't know how they do it—mask the adrenaline, play it cool.

I can't keep focus. I'm not the heartless automaton I thought I could be. I pictured myself coming here, entirely determined and lethal. Instead, I'm pretending not to desperately fight off paranoia as it slays me with a million possible pitfalls to our plan.

"Get moving, shorty." Luca keeps his expression impassive, not giving me a hint to his emotions. "We've got eyes on us from the front door."

I don't look. Don't nod.

"Ready?" His gaze bores into me, intense and filled with concern.

I give a subtle incline of my head and follow his lead toward the house. I stiffen when his gentle grip glides over the crook of my elbow, but it's too late to warn him of his mistake. Two guards exit the front of the mansion—Argus and Otis—both of them looking down at where Luca holds my arm.

"You shouldn't be touching her." Argus places the butt of his rifle on the ground, his pinched brows pulled tight.

"I know." Luca tugs me forward. "But she's a feisty little thing and I didn't want her attempting to run again."

"She tried to escape?"

"Tried. Failed. Got punished." Luca stops us before

them and releases his gentle grip to run a taunting hand through my hair. "Didn't you, pretty Penny?"

I shudder.

His touch is kind… but those words… that name.

The provocation from his lips shakes me to my core.

I jerk my head away. "Merely keeping you on your toes, asshole."

He drops his hand from my hair to reclaim my arm. "You learned your lesson though, didn't you? And if you attempt that stupidity again, nothing will save you."

I suck in a breath at how real his threat sounds. How sickening. Then his finger gently strokes the inside of my arm, the delicate brush in contrast to his vicious words.

He's trying to comfort me. Attempting to ease his flawless act with a reaffirming touch.

I appreciate it. I appreciate *him*.

I don't want to. *God*, how I don't want to, but I do.

"So, let's get this party started." Hunter claps his hands together. "Point us in the direction of the women. I'm ready to see what all the fuss is about."

Otis starts for the mansion doors when a grunt of muted sound disturbs the night air from the yard. It's a noise of death that isn't entirely discreet.

Argus must hear it too because he stiffens, his focus shifting to the darkness over my shoulder. "What was that?" He raises his wrist, preparing to speak into his comms device.

Holy shit.

I break out in a cold sweat, certain our attack is about to be discovered.

"I heard it, too." Luca turns toward the yard, stepping

closer to me, increasing the brush of his finger. "Want us to check it out?"

I stop breathing.

One wrong move…

One suspicious word…

One instruction into that communication device and my sisters are dead.

"No." Argus inches toward the driveway, his lips pressed to the mouthpiece in his palm. "Can we get—"

Luca lunges, landing a left hook to Argus's cheek, his other hand gripping the rifle. He yanks the weapon forward, sending the guard stumbling while Hunter lashes out at Otis, pummeling with one fist then the other.

I scramble backward, stepping out of the way as my protectors attack with brutal efficiency. The guards don't have a chance to retaliate. They drop. From knees, to palms, to stomachs.

It's such beautiful savagery.

That is, until the sound of gunfire erupts from inside and my brief sense of optimism vanishes in a punishing heartbeat.

11

LUCA

I slam the guard down on the cement as gunfire explodes inside. The screams of women follow.

Penny's friends are in trouble.

I shoot Hunt a glance, his ferocity meeting mine for a brief second before he lands a vicious kick to the guard laying before him, his boot making a direct jaw hit. Otis falls limp. Out like a light.

I'm not as kind. I drop to my knees, grab my blubbering enemy around the head, and break his neck with a swift jerk of my hands.

"Where is she?" Decker speaks into my earpiece. "Where's Penny?"

I scramble to my feet, snatch the rifle along the way to point it toward the sound of approaching steps.

It's Deck, his eyes filled with fury as he yanks two pistols from the back of his waistband. "Where the fuck is she?"

I drop the rifle, catch the weapon he lobs at me, then

turn to find her. "She's…" I keep turning, not seeing her anywhere.

"Fuck. She must have slipped by me." Hunt snatches the second thrown pistol and makes for the mansion doors. "I'll get her."

"No." Decker rushes in front of him. "There's still one more guard outside. You take care of it. I'm going after my sister." He doesn't pause for confirmation as he shoves his way past Hunter to disappear inside.

"I'm going with him." I follow, stopping beside Hunt to hand over the car key. "Put Otis in the trunk. We'll need him later."

I maneuver inside the mansion, turning down the hall to the right as Decker runs in a crouch along the left.

I pass doorways, giving each room a cursory glance, my gun aimed and ready as I panic over finding Penny. She can't have gone far. She was right there. By my fucking side one minute and gone the next.

I don't stop my search until shouts carry from around the corner of the hall. I slow, quietening my steps as I lean close to the wall and chance a glance around the edge.

There's a guard a few yards away, his rifle pointed toward an open doorway, his aim low. "Get up, bitch."

Fuck. It could be Penny.

I shoot, blasting the motherfucker in the head to plaster his blood over a nearby painting, his limp body flopping to the floor.

More screams lash the air, the closest coming from that open doorway, the sound quickly smothered. There's the shout of men from another corner of the house. The thud of a struggle, too.

I creep toward the room, stepping over the dead guard, and chance a glance inside the darkened interior.

"Penny?" I blink to adjust to the lack of light and find three bunks. A dresser. A closet. But no warrior woman, only the faintest hint of movement from the far corner. "Shorty, is that you?"

I crouch slowly, the movement incremental, my gun still at the ready. "Are you in here?" I flatten onto my stomach, doing a visual sweep under the beds to find two wide eyes beaming back at me from under the farthest bunk.

It's another woman, her body shrouded in darkness.

I place down my weapon and tilt my hands skyward. "I'm here to help."

She doesn't move. Doesn't blink.

"My name's Luca. I was here the other day with Cole."

Still, no movement. No noise.

"Stay where you are, okay? I'll come back for you once it's safe." I reclaim my gun and brace to stand. "Have you seen Penny? Did she walk by?"

Her hesitation continues for long seconds before she finally nods. It's barely there. Almost unseen.

"Did she continue down the hall?"

This time her nod is more defined. Adamant.

"Okay. Good." I shove to my feet, thankful for the adrenaline faintly masking the pounding in my skull. Those gunshots messed with my head. The attack on the guard did, too.

I reclaim my position close to the wall and continue into uncharted territory, my vision not entirely at the top of its game. I have to blink to make things crystal, and that's a fucking worry all on its own.

"*Penny?*" I yell. "Where are you?"

A thunder of footsteps sound from the hall I just trekked. Not light. Not hers. As soon as the asshole comes around the corner, I shoot.

Pop. Pop.

He crumples. It's too fucking easy. And it's entirely fucking clear these guards aren't guards at all. They're puppets armed with the least tactical weapon on earth to be used indoors.

Their lack of skill doesn't make sense. Unless Luther truly was untouchable out here and these guards are for show.

"I've taken down two." I speak into the microphone hidden under my shirt. "But something doesn't feel right."

Someone grunts, the sound resembling a struggle.

More gunfire erupts, the noise carrying from outside.

"One more down." Hunt pants through my earpiece. "But Penny must've got her count wrong. I can still hear someone else out here."

Pop. Pop. Pop.

This time the shots ricochet from inside, the brain-piercing noise vibrating off the walls to tamper my ability to distinguish the location.

Women wail. A male shouts.

"Penny," someone cries. "*Penny.*"

I run, taking the first archway on my left to dart and weave through a dining room.

"Tadd, you don't want to do this."

It's her, the familiar voice carrying from nearby.

I don't stop. Don't even pause. I sprint toward the sound and skitter to a halt when I find her standing in an archway, her arms raised in surrender, light from inside the room bathing her in an ethereal glow.

"Penny, don't go in there." I keep running. Scrambling.

She ignores me to step out of view.

Pop. Pop.

I die at the sound of those shots. The accompanying screams are brutal. Gunfire takes over—from the other side of the house and outside. It's everywhere, the thunder pounding into my skull.

I push harder, sprinting into the unknown a few feet behind her, yelling a war cry in the hopes of stealing the attention of any threat toward her. As soon as I breach the room, shots rain down on me from an asshole with a rifle. I dive, the whistle of a bullet brushing my ear as I sail through the air, my gun steady.

I return fire—*pop, pop*—then hit the ground hard, the smooth tile helping me to slide behind the safety of a sofa.

For a second, I lie there, waiting for a lethal wound to announce itself, listening for movement of an enemy as blackness spots over my vision.

There's more screaming. More sobbing.

But no more fire.

The battle dies for a moment.

"Penny?" I struggle to raise to my elbows. *"Penny?"* I shove to my feet, cautious, and find the guard, barely in his twenties, dead on the floor.

Penny stands a few yards to his left, two more women close by her side, and another spread on the floor at her feet, her body and face shielded by the legs standing around her.

I edge my way toward them as I take in my surroundings—the floor-to-ceiling windows providing no protection from an outside threat, another archway at the far side of the room, and the extravagant furniture capable of hiding an enemy.

"It's okay." Penny collapses to her knees beside the prone figure, the other two women following suit from the opposite side of the motionless body. "You're going to be okay."

"Was she hit?" I back toward them, my gun and sight shifting between the open doorways. "Talk to me."

My answer comes in the form of slowly building sobs. First one woman, then another.

"In the stomach," Penny whispers. "She needs to get to a hospital."

Fuck.

There are no hospitals. Not for this type of situation.

"Hunt, Deck, I've found them. But I need you guys to give me an update." I reach Penny's side and peer down at the woman on the floor who's barely a woman at all, her face seeming more like an innocent child's.

"I've got one asshole playing hide-n-seek over here," Decker says. "But I think that's the last of them on my side of the house."

"One got away," Hunt adds. "He scaled the fucking wall."

"Did he see your fucking face?" I ask.

"Doubt it. The little bitch was running scared. I'm tempted to run after him."

"No. We've gotta get out of here, and I'm going to need help moving these women." Three of them at least. And the fourth who I left in the nearby bedroom. The fifth won't be going anywhere.

There's no saving her.

Blood seeps across the material of her silken nightwear, the building gurgle in her throat announcing the stream of liquid death about to spill from her lips.

Penny presses her hands to the woman's abdomen, placing pressure on the wound. "We're going to get you out of here, Chloe. We're free."

There's confidence in her voice.

Unwarranted, unwavering confidence.

"She's going to start choking." I indicate for the blonde to move to the left with a jut of my gun. "Get behind her and lift her shoulders."

Her trepidatious gaze darts between me and Penny before she finally scrambles to her knees to raise Chloe's head onto her lap. Not that her compliance matters. The injured woman coughs, the first burst of blood spluttering from her mouth.

"Hold on," Penny demands. "Keep fighting."

More blood bubbles across porcelain skin, the gagging and choking increasing.

The two other women sob. Cry. Hyperventilate.

But Penny doesn't lose her determination. She keeps pressing on Chloe's wound, her fingers drowning in blood as the spluttering loses its ferocity, the wide eyes of the dying girl growing dull.

"Chloe," Penny warns. "Stay with me."

There's nothing I can do, not one fucking thing, as Chloe's soul quickly slips from her body. She gurgles with the blood suffocating her, her shoulders twitching, once, twice. Then she's gone, her head slumping limp, the red stream of death still dripping from her innocent lips.

The other women wail, grasping at the deceased's hands and face.

They beg. They plead. They sob.

All Penny does is stiffen.

There are no tears or weakness. She doesn't show one ounce of vulnerability as she stares unblinking at her fallen sister.

The gunshot echoing from the other side of the house doesn't even make her jolt. It's the other women who scream and scramble to their feet to run for cover as heavy footfalls approach from the hall.

I step in front of Penny, shielding her, and aim my gun. A figure invades the doorway, tempting my trigger finger.

"It's me," Decker calls, withdrawing from view. "Don't shoot." He waits a heartbeat then re-enters as more thunderous steps carry toward us. "Hunter's behind me."

He takes in the sight before him with apprehension, his gaze sliding over the newest additions to our crew before settling on the corpse on the floor. "Is she dead?"

I nod. "Bullet to the gut."

Hunter storms into the room, his attention following the same path as Decker's. "We've gotta get out of here. The asshole who escaped could be calling backup."

"Did we get any intel?" Decker asks. "Have the safes been checked?"

"There's no time. I'm not willing to risk it." I start for Penny and jut my chin toward the two other women cowering on the floor. "Hunt, you help them. Deck, you get back outside and grab the duffels. We can't leave anything behind."

Decker eyes me, then Penny. He's about to make another comment about me getting between him and his sister, and I don't have the fucking patience.

"If I knew where you put the duffels I'd get them myself," I growl, "but I don't. So get your ass moving."

He glares, making me well aware I'll be paying for my actions later.

I don't fucking care. We need to move.

"Ladies, it's time to leave." Hunter starts toward them as Decker jogs from the room. "It's not safe here."

I don't wait to watch their reactions. I keep my focus on Penny, who remains at Chloe's side, her hands still pressed into the pool of blood on the woman's abdomen.

"Shorty…" I walk up behind her to crouch at her back. "We need to get moving."

She doesn't acknowledge me. Doesn't budge an inch as her attention remains riveted on the woman staring unblinking at the roof.

"Pen?" I brush her arm. "We need to go."

There's no sound. Nothing. She's emotionless. Catatonic.

"Come on." Hunter raises his voice. "You want to go home, don't you?"

"Home?" one of the women ask.

"Yes, home." Hunter claps his hands as if trying to gain the attention of school children. "We've gotta go."

The two women climb to their feet together, hand in hand.

"Penny?" the blonde asks.

She doesn't answer. Doesn't even flinch.

"It's okay. I've got her. We won't be far behind you." I turn my attention to Hunter. "I'm going to need to get her cleaned up. There's too much blood."

It's all over her hands. Her legs, too. She can't walk back through the Naxos port like this.

"Can you handle her on your own?"

"I'm good." I glide my grip around Penny's wrists and gently guide her away from Chloe. "There's another woman left hiding in one of the bedrooms. I'll get her to help. Just make sure you grab that fucker out of the trunk and put him into the backseat. If he's not awake, there's smelling salts in one of the duffels. And you're also going to need to get him to swallow some of the liquid E I've got stashed in there, too. We need to make him look like he's drunk, not a fucking prisoner, when we haul him to the boat."

He grins. "My pleasure." He turns for the door. "Come on, ladies. Let's get you home."

After a few moments of tear-stained contemplation, the women follow, leaving Penny behind with me.

I guess I should be thankful for their compliance. But I'm not. I'm fucking bitter they only spared a few seconds for Penny's concern when left with a stranger, after she put everything on the line to save them.

She fought for those women. She begged and threatened.

And they've walked away from her.

"Come on, shorty." I rub her wrists. "The worst is over."

She's still unmoving. Not even nudging out of her shock.

Fuck it.

I wrap an arm around her back and the other under her knees to lift her off the ground. She doesn't fight, barely gives a muted whimper as I carry her through the dining room, into the hall to the darkened bedroom with the three bunks.

"Are you still in here?" I place Penny on her feet. "It's safe to come out."

There's a rustle of movement as the woman crawls from under the bed. She's another wide-eyed innocent, her pain trapped behind generous beauty. "Penny?"

"Help me get her cleaned up. Can you get me some fresh clothes and a wet cloth?"

She nods, the movement jerky, before she hustles to the closet.

"You're going to be okay." I brush Penny's arms, trying to rub away the chill of shock as I lean in. Eye to eye. "You're strong. You can get through this."

She meets my gaze, sorrow thick in her dark irises.

"Here." The other woman returns with a thick layer of white material in her hands. "It's her favorite dress."

"Thanks." I take the offering, ignoring how inappropriate a frilly, feminine dress is at a moment like this, and fling the clothing over my shoulder.

"Let me help." The other woman moves closer, protectively nudging me out of the way as she makes easy work of Penny's oversized T-shirt, raising the hem from her thighs to expose pure nudity.

Holy. Shit.

Decker's sister is entirely naked under that shirt. No panties. No bra. Only smooth, perfect skin marred with sinister bruises along her hips and inner thighs. My gaze latches on to those marks—the sickening implications, the fucking brutality—as the other woman scrambles to cover Penny again, lifting the dress over her head.

"Wait." I halt her with a raise of my hand and quickly turn off the microphone around my neck. "Where's her underwear?"

She shakes her head. "We're not allowed." She doesn't pause as she helps guide Penny's head through the material.

"Wait," I repeat with barely leashed frustration. *Fuck.* I'm getting pummeled here. Visually. Verbally. The muttered conversation through my earpiece along with the approaching freight train of a migraine is making it hard to think. "She can't put on a fucking white dress when her hands are covered in blood. I'm going to need that cloth. *Now.*"

The woman retreats at my anger, her hands trembling.

"I'm not going to hurt her. Just get me that cloth. We need to get out of here."

She straightens her shoulders and nods, leaving me alone with the most heartbreakingly gorgeous woman I've ever laid eyes on.

"Penny..." *Fuck me.* I don't know what to say. I don't even know where to look as she stares at the floor.

"Chloe..." The name is whispered from her lips. "She's gone."

"I know." I shove my gun into my waistband, loosen the brain-numbing comm device in my ear so Hunt and Decker's voices stop punishing me, and reach for the nearest bed to tug off the coverings. "I'm sorry." I grab her wrist, needing to busy myself with something other than visual violation, and wipe the blood from her fingers. "You've been dealt a rough fucking hand, sweetheart. I can't imagine what you're going through."

I stroke her skin, over and over, sweeping away layer upon layer of death. "You're going to be okay." I keep my gaze trained on her arms as I utter the placation. In honesty, I have no idea if she'll physically make it through, let alone mentally. "Once we get you home, you're going to be fine."

She shudders out a breath, the warmth brushing my face.

I want nothing more than to wrap her in cotton wool. To shelter her. To slay every sick son of a bitch who dared to witness her suffering only to turn a blind eye.

"Lilly..." Penny blinks to awareness when the other woman re-enters the room, her trance of grief lessening the slightest fraction. "It's good to see you."

"It's good to see you, too." The other woman hands the cloth to me while her attention remains on Penny's arms. "Is that your blood? Are you hurt?"

"No. It's—"

Shit. "Lilly, I need you to go outside and find the others." She has to remain ignorant. I can't risk any more theatrical delays. "Tell them we're almost ready."

"But I want to stay with—"

"It's okay, Lil." Penny's voice is hollow. "Find the others. We won't be long."

I keep my attention on the cleanup as Lilly reluctantly backtracks from the room. I wipe Penny's wrists, her palms, in between her fingers.

"I can do that myself." She attempts to pull her hand away, but I cling tight, needing to remain tethered.

"I'm sure you could." I give a half-hearted grin. "But would you do as good a job as me?"

"Luca." My name is part plea, part exhausted warning. "I can do it."

"What did I say about listening, shorty?" I grab her other arm and begin the same ritual.

Soon, she'll be on her way out of this nightmare, and

I'll be stuck thinking I didn't do enough to help her. That I left her in Luther's clutches when I shouldn't have. That I caused her more pain than necessary.

This is the least I can do. Mere swipes of a damp cloth over delicate skin. Bit by bit I clean away the blood, wishing I was cleaning away her suffering.

"I…" She lets out a long breath. "I think I blacked out in there. Or…" She sighs and shakes her head in confusion. "I don't know. I'm so tired."

"It's shock." I make quick work of her other arm, trying to remain gentle as her nudity taunts me. I can't stop myself from taking a glimpse. But it's not for pleasure. It's because of those fucking marks. "Those bruises…?" I can't finish my question. It's not the time or place to voice my angered curiosity when it's clear who marked her. "I'm sorry. I didn't mean to look."

"The exposure means nothing to me anymore," she whispers. "I lost ownership of my body long ago."

I clench my jaw. Tight.

Anger clogs my throat. Rage burns my veins.

I wipe the last of the blood from her hand, throw the cloth to the floor, and help drag the material from around her neck to cover her nudity. "Nobody owns you. Not Luther. Not his men."

"You don't understand." She busies herself righting the dress, her attention downcast. "You've got no idea."

"Then tell me."

She shakes her head.

"*Tell me.*"

She stiffens, her frantic gaze raising to mine. "Luther may be dead but his shackles still enslave me. There's no escaping what he did. He'll always own me."

"I fucking disagree."

"I wish I had your optimism. I guess it's true that ignorance is bliss."

Her argument is solid, but I refuse to fucking believe it. There's no way this woman can't bounce back. There's too much life left in her to give up now.

"We'll discuss this later." I grab her hand and lead her from the room, stepping over the dead guy in the hall. We reach the front door together, then as soon as Penny makes her way outside she stumbles forward to her friends. The other women are already crying, their sobs increasing tenfold as Penny engulfs them in a group hug.

"What the fuck took so long?" Decker storms toward me. "We need to figure out what we're doing."

"What do you mean?" I frown at Hunter as he approaches. "I thought the plan was to get straight back to the island."

"That was the original plan." He stops before me, one hand clutching his gun, the other raking through his hair. "But these women aren't stable. They haven't stopped crying to take a fucking breath. And you and I both know Torian won't be able to cope with that drama. He needs to focus to finish what you came here for. So it's best if we get them out of here now."

"I've already spoken to Torian," Decker adds, "and he agrees. He's going to make a call to the pilots and also find a way off this island via a private dock. It's less dangerous that way, seeing as though only one of us is going with them."

This is bullshit. Fucking bullshit. "You haven't thought this through. Penny can't leave."

Hunter raises a brow. "She can't? Or you don't want her to?"

I get in his face and smile. Laugh. I try to fake a disregard to his assumption even though it hits too close to home. "If you were smart, you'd remember the fight she put up just because she wanted to bring the kid on this little escapade. So if you try to send her to another country without him, you're going to have full-blown hysteria on your hands. *Contagious fucking hysteria.* Which means instead of four blubbering messes, you're going to have a group of inconsolable trouble."

"Then she can stay." Hunter shrugs. "From what I've seen she hasn't shed a tear anyway. It's the others who need to go."

"And who the fuck is going with them? They can't make that trip on their own."

"I guess that depends if Penny stays or goes. If she remains in Greece I assume lover boy—" he jerks his chin at me "—and big brother will want to keep hovering close. That leaves me to do the heavy lifting, because don't forget that asshole who got away could be planning any number of things."

I clench my teeth, biting back a reply to his "lover boy" comment that will only strengthen his derisive argument.

"It's the best option," Decker grates. "Hunt can go back and—"

He stops mid-sentence at the sound of crunching pebbles behind him. It's Penny, her fragile frame coming to stand a few feet away.

"I heard my name." She inches closer. "What's going on?"

Hunt clears his throat. Decker glances off in the

distance while rubbing the back of his neck. Both of them act as if they didn't hear her question, making it fucking clear they expect me to be the bearer of temperamental news.

"Fuck you," I mutter under my breath, then walk to stand in front of her. "We're changing things up a little. It's for the best if we get your friends on a jet and send them home right away."

"What do you mean right away?"

"He means now. From here, to a boat, to the airport." Hunt speaks up. "You need to decide if you're staying or going."

Her eyes flare in shock, those dark depths cutting me down at the knees. "Without going back to the island to collect Tobias?"

"Yes." I nod. "Torian has already organized the jet."

Her lips part and her already pale skin turns ashen. "Then I'm staying. I won't leave Toby behind."

Decker winces. "You'd be safer—"

"I don't care what's safe. I'm not leaving without him. He's just a little boy."

"And what about your friends?" I ask. "You're happy for them to go without you."

"No, Luca, I'm not happy," she scolds. "But you've given me no choice."

A tense second of silence falls between us.

I don't want to do this to her. It's not fucking ideal. But those eyes hold me accountable. The glimmer of betrayal cuts me to the core.

"Okay, if that's settled, we need to make a move." Hunter starts for the other women. "Say your goodbyes."

"Jesus Christ," I mutter. "Have some fucking sympathy."

"Wait up." Decker follows after him. "I need to tell you where I hid the car."

They leave me alone with her pained judgment. Penny continues to stare back at me, her exhausted sorrow forever tattooing my mind.

"You're really doing this?" Her nose wrinkles as if she's trying to dislodge the tingle of building tears. "They're not strong enough to go without me."

"You don't need to mother them anymore." It's obvious Penny has been their rock. She was the one they turned to with questions of my sincerity. The three others took a step back at every opportunity when Penny rushed forward to save them. "Hunter can take care of it. He'll make sure they arrive in the States safely."

"They won't like that."

"Then convince them. Or go with them. It's your choice."

Penny's eyes remain hardened, but the severity loses its edge. She's exhausted. Bone-deep. "I can't leave Tobias with those people. Not when I know what they're capable of."

"Then, like Hunt said, say your goodbyes." I try my fucking hardest not to let her vulnerability wear me down. "You'll see them again soon enough."

She sighs, the breath of defeat punishingly brittle before she returns to her friends. She talks in a low murmur, her undecipherable words causing the women to erupt in more tears, their arms wrapping around her as they sob against her shoulders.

She clings to them, her fingers white-knuckled, but still

she doesn't break. There're only strong eyes that hold mine as if begging for this new form of torture to stop.

She's been through murder, death, reunion, salvation, and now a farewell all in one day, and she hasn't shed a single tear. Not one. Any sane, full-grown man would have blubbered through the experience.

"Come on." I start for the car. "I need to get the fuck out of here."

12

PENNY

I walk on numb feet from the car to the start of the Naxos port, Luca at my side as he carries the duffels while Sebastian is up ahead, his arm wrapped around the guard who stumbles along at his side.

They gave him something. Ecstasy or speed maybe. I don't know. But the effects make the man appear drunk. He's swaying, not protesting as my brother slurs out a rendition of *"Fifty-Five Bottles of Beer on the Wall"* to increase the ruse that we're not taking one of Luther's men as a prisoner.

Yet all I see is Chloe.

I stagger along the pier, each blink punishing me with a snapshot of her suffering.

I climb into the boat as guilt consumes me, the fact I'm alive while she's dead is so bitterly unfair.

And when I take a seat on the cushioned bench and stare at Otis, who Sebastian shoves to the floor, all I want to do is make the guard pay.

I need his dried blood under my nails, not Chloe's.

I yearn to see the fear of death in his eyes, just like I had to witness in hers.

I crave the euphoria of hurting him, punishing him, torturing him. Because that's what they did to her.

To *all* of us.

His future suffering is what I focus on as my brother starts the boat and guides us from the port. But Otis doesn't suffer. He's not even scared. Whatever they gave him has plastered a delirious smile on his face, the expression pure evil.

I can't stand it.

Chloe is gone—left on the cold floor in a pool of her own blood, her soul forever trapped in that godforsaken house—and this man is blissed out.

It makes me sick.

I drag my gaze away and turn to the water, wishing the excruciatingly slow journey would pass faster. The minutes tick by like hours, the muted chuckle from the maniac on the floor a constant grate on my ears.

"You're dead, pretty Penny. They're going to eat you alive."

I ache at his words. Shiver. It isn't from fear, though. It's from suffocating anger. Every emotion bottled inside me has been increased tenfold—the grief, resentment, hatred, heartache and sorrow. I need to make it stop, I just don't know how.

"You're going to wish you never defied Luther," he slurs. "They're going to make you pay."

I close my eyes and pray for calm.

"You'll beg for death."

I swing around and lean toward him, inching closer,

resting my elbows on my knees. "And who, exactly, is going to do all this to me?"

He beams a bright smile, his eyes lazily blinking. "Robert. You know Luther promised you to him. And the things he's going to do to you…" He laughs and flops onto his back, gyrating his hips to the night sky. "You will probably love it. Just like you loved everything Luther put you through."

I gasp. My throat constricts.

"You think I enjoyed what Luther did to me?" I can't keep the shock from my voice.

"You give him exactly what he wants because you love the dick. We all know. Luther does, too. He laughs about how pathetic you are."

He's serious. He truly believes I enjoyed the torture.

"That's why you stayed the longest. Luther loves that you love him."

"Well, Luther's dead." I burst to my feet, about to plant my foot into his ribs. "Robert, Chris, Tadd, Argus, and all the rest, too. And you're next."

"Hey." Luca starts toward me, cutting me off before I reach my target. "What's going on?"

"It's not true." I attempt to walk around him, to get to Otis, only to have the wall of muscle sidestep into my path. "He's wrong."

"Wrong about what?"

I shake my head, my cheeks heating. I can't repeat the conversation. I don't want anyone to even question what I did. How I survived. But my depraved strategy haunts me. I *did* give Luther what he wanted. I worked hard to make sure I was his favorite.

"Don't let him get to you." Luca steps closer, his hands

reaching toward my arms.

I bat away his touch. "Don't let him get to me?" I keep repeating those words in my head, but can't quit the resentment that follows. Luca is asking for the impossible. Otis is already under my skin, his toxicity speeding through my veins.

"He's taunting me." My voice cracks. "He's practically laughing at me."

"That's the drugs. Things will change once we get him back to Torian."

I'm not appeased. Not in the slightest. Setting Otis on fire, one slow inch at a time, wouldn't give me enough satisfaction. "What will you do to him?"

"Whatever necessary to get information."

Information.

Shit.

"I-I was meant to help you find Luther's office. And the safes," I ramble, trying to drown out more regret. "I forgot."

"Don't worry. We'll get this fucker to talk. He'll give us a lead or two." He jerks his head toward the bench seat. "You should sit down and rest."

How can I sit when the scum of the earth thinks I enjoyed my punishments? How could I possibly rest with those accusations hanging over my head?

God. I feel so dirty. So worthless.

I turn away, dragging my feet to the back of the boat to stare across the inky black. It would be too easy to jump over the edge with one of those duffels tangled around my feet. I'd drown, the death not coming quickly or painlessly, but at least my suffering would soon be over.

There would be no more taunts of illusive freedom.

I'd finally escape this hellish existence.

"She's a fucking whore." Otis's voice raises over the purr of the boat. "A dead whore."

I close my eyes and wrap my arms around my middle, the weight of Luca and Sebastian's judgment on my shoulders.

I don't flinch at the thud that sounds moments later, or the cry of masculine pain.

"Ignore him, Penny," my brother demands. "Just fucking ignore him."

I try my best, but the alternate thoughts lying in wait are all about Chloe. About death and fear and failure.

By the time we reach Torian's island, I want to vomit. Bile teases the back of my throat. The only thing stopping me from falling to my knees is the knowledge I won't have the strength to get back up.

I remain in place as Otis is hauled to his feet and dragged onto the jetty. I don't follow when Luca calls out, "Are you coming?"

"In a minute." I need more time. Maybe a lifetime.

He nods, his focus already on retribution as he helps Sebastian drag the guard along the trail to the mansion, all three of them quickly disappearing from sight.

I stay there, alone in the silence, blanketed in darkness.

Is this what freedom feels like? Is it the tightness of pure isolation? The punishing weight of guilt? The acidic taste of failure?

Otis implied I remained in Luther's house because they thought I was a joke. They laughed at my actions. They knew I was willing to sleep with my rapist, but they didn't spare a thought as to the reason why. Maybe nobody else will, either.

I dig my fingernails into my palms, pressing harder and deeper, attempting to lessen the emotional torment with something physical. When that doesn't help, I climb from the boat and use the sharp pebbles of the trail to punish me from my soles upward.

I walk with hard steps, increasing the pain. I stomp. I twist. I don't stop until the faint shriek of male torture leaves me motionless.

For a second, my excruciating thoughts cease, my suffering placed on pause.

My breath remains trapped in my lungs as I wait for more of that rewarding sound. My heart pounds with yearning. My palms sweat with impatience.

I have to hear that cry again. I want Otis to wail and scream and blubber. I need it to help ease my anguish.

I run for the house in search of the sweet comfort, sprinting around the pool to pull the glass door wide.

Keira waits in the kitchen, her eyes widening at the sight of me. "Are you okay?"

I ignore her in my trek for the hall.

"Wait." She hustles after me, cutting me off before I reach the archway. "What happened? Nobody has told me anything. Did your friends get to safety? I overheard Cole—"

"Three of my sisters are on their way home."

She huffs out a relieved breath. "I'm so glad to hear it."

"*Three,*" I repeat. "When there were five of us. Not to mention all those who died previously at your father's command."

Her relaxation vanishes. "I'm so—"

"I wish I had a definitive number to give to you because I'm sure you guys have some sort of family death tally, but I gave up counting a few months after I arrived."

"Penny, I…"

"What?" I raise my brows. "You're sorry?"

"Yes. I'm sorry. For everything."

"Do you feel sorry when you're putting on your designer clothes? Or those expensive shoes? Because you know where your family's money came from, right?"

She pulls back, clearly offended.

"And are you sorry when you're sleeping with the man whose family you destroyed? Are you sorry when you're fucking my brother?"

"Penny." She raises her hands in placation. "I didn't do anything wrong. We didn't know what was happening here and as soon as we found out we took action."

"You found out three days ago?" I wave away my heavy sarcasm, not entirely sure why I'm trying to pick a fight. This woman means nothing to me. I don't care what she says or thinks. All I want from her is instructions on how to find Otis. I need directions to help stop the insanity beating down on me. "Do I turn left or right down the hall to find them?"

"Please don't blame me." Her face crumples. "I haven't gotten through this unscathed either. We're all suffering. Some more than others."

I should have *triggered* tattooed on my forehead for the number of buttons she simultaneously pressed. "Wow."

"Listen." She reaches for me, then thinks better of it, her hand falling to her side. "The perversions weren't contained to the Greek islands. They happened at home, too. And I was a victim."

It's my turn to pull back, my retreat made in confusion.

"What sort of victim?"

"One like you. I was only a child when I lost my innocence to a man."

"Luther?" The name whispers from my lips.

"No. Not my father. But it was someone he knew was a monster and he allowed them access to me anyway."

My punishment increases. The anger I had for her moments before escapes in a vacuum. One minute, it's there. The next, it's gone, being replaced by more choking guilt.

Every time I think I've become accustomed to how shocking the crimes of men can be, the world teaches me differently. I'm repeatedly shown that there's no escaping the misery.

"What I was put through is nothing in comparison to what you've endured." She holds my gaze, now backing away from my scrutiny. "But I'm not clueless to your suffering. And I struggle every day knowing I could've put a stop to it sooner if I didn't think I was the only one. So I'm sorry." Her eyes begin to water as she sucks in a deep breath. "I'm sorry for my ignorance… I'm sorry for the actions of my father…" Her lips begin to tremble. "And I'm sorry for falling in love with your brother, but Sebastian is the one who saved me, and I'm sure he can do the same for you if only you'd let him."

Goosebumps skitter over my skin, every inch of me touched by her words.

I don't know what to say. I'm not strong enough to apologize to the daughter of my rapist, no matter the severity of her plight.

She gives me a sad smile through the awkward silence. "Would you like something to eat?" Keira doesn't wait for a response. She turns and walks for the kitchen, the muted sound of torture continuing to carry down the hall. "Tobias woke while you were gone. He asked about you."

Tobias.

Oh, God. For a moment, I'd completely forgotten about him, my thoughts entirely selfish. "Was he scared?"

"No. Mostly curious. He sat with me for a while. I made him hot cocoa and told him about his family in Portland. He seems like a good kid."

"He *is* a good kid." The muffled cries grow louder, the sweet promise of retribution plaguing me. "Did he go back to sleep?"

"He did. But I'm not sure how long he will stay that way with all the noise."

I cringe, knowing exactly how much that little boy can sleep through. His slumber could withstand the suffering of me and my sisters on a nightly basis. The current muffled cries are nothing in comparison.

"What is it?" she asks. "What are you thinking?"

"Nothing." I shake my head, but I'm unable to break free of the memories as I continue for the hall. Living nightmares blur my vision. The beatings. The restraints.

"Penny, wait."

I don't listen. I reach the hall and turn left into unmarked territory as her quickened footsteps give chase.

"You can't go in there." She rushes after me, stalking at my back as I pass door upon door, the wails building. "You don't want to see what they're doing."

I stop before the last door. The one that carries the blissful sounds. "Yes, I do." I want to see it. Remember it. Breathe it deep.

She squeezes in front of me, blocking my path. "I'm

sorry. I can't let you in there."

"Are you sure?" I hold her gaze. "Because I thought we finally reached common ground."

"I'm trying to shield you from what's happening."

"And why is it that everyone seems to think they know what's best for me? First Luca, then Sebastian, now you. I've witnessed unimaginable things. Traumatic, disgusting things that will forever be stuck in my head. And yet you think I can't handle seeing a little torture? That I'm not owed the gift of his suffering?"

She doesn't answer. Doesn't move either.

"Get out of my way, Keira." I nudge closer. "Don't crack the fragile ground we stand on."

"God damn it." She steps to the side.

I push through the door to a soulless exercise room. It takes a few short seconds for another shout to tell me the men must be in the sauna in the far corner.

"Please be careful." Keira continues to follow. "They won't want to be disturbed."

"I don't care what they want." I yank open the wooden door to four sets of eyes turning my way. Cole sits on the wooden bench, leaned back, relaxed, while Sebastian and Luca loom over the bloodied man roped to a chair. Otis's eyes are now swollen and red with his naked chest marked with a hundred tiny cuts.

He's become unrecognizable in such a short space of time. So beautifully, brutally foreign.

"Can I help you?" Cole raises a brow.

Sebastian steps back from the man in the chair, his knuckles stained with blood. The tight pinch of his face speaks of shame. *My* shame. Otis must have told him something.

"What did he say?" I inch farther into the small space.

I get no response. Luca doesn't look at me. Sebastian turns away. It's only Torian who pays me attention.

"What did he say?" I ask him. "What did he tell you about me?"

"Does it matter? We're not here for a history lesson. We're only interested in shutting down my father's operation."

"Cole," Keira warns. "Don't be heartless."

He gives a tight smile. "Forgive me, sister. I assure you he hasn't said much."

Not much. But still something.

My heart clenches at the possibilities. I don't want them knowing. I can't stand the thought of them having access to the intimate details of my shame. It's too much. I can't breathe.

"He's only talking shit to waste time." Luca turns to face me, his eyes wild and animalistic. "He may have thought bad-mouthing you was a good idea. I taught him otherwise."

"What did he say?" I step closer. "What did he tell you?"

His mouth presses into a tight line, his jaw ticking as he wipes sweat from his brow with his forearm. "Nothing helpful."

"I told them you liked it, bitch," Otis sneers. "You fucking loved it. We all knew."

My eyes burn. My throat, too.

He told them. He repeated the lies from earlier.

"You should get out of here." Luca indicates the door with a wave of his hand. "Go on."

"It's not true." I shake my head, my hands trembling,

my heart tapping out an erratic beat. "You can't believe him."

"Of course we don't fucking believe him." Luca steps into me, backing me toward the door. "We know it's not true."

The cringe on Sebastian's face says otherwise. His expression is the definition of judgment.

"I'm not leaving." I stand my ground, not retreating despite his approach. "Let me watch."

"No." Sebastian's denial is adamant. "Go back to Tobias. He shouldn't be left alone."

"He's asleep. And I have a right to be here." I speak to Luca. "Please."

He remains close. So close his warmth soothes the icy chill inside me.

"*Please*," I beg.

Tortured heartbeats pass until Otis begins to chuckle.

"See? She's a needy little bitch, isn't she?"

Luca turns, his fist connecting with the guard's stomach. Otis hunches, his laughter continuing as he gasps and coughs.

"She stays," Luca commands to no one in particular. "She has a right to watch him suffer."

My stomach twists at his support. Flips and tangles alongside the tumultuous mix of my emotions.

"Fine." Cole crosses his feet at the ankles. "But keep out of the way."

"But she likes to be in the thick of it," Otis slurs. "Don't you, pretty Penny? You're all about the thickness."

My fingers twitch, demanding action. I struggle not to let him affect me as I walk to the bench seat and sit rigid a foot away from Cole.

"Get out of here, china doll." Sebastian walks to the door, blocking Keira from moving inside. "You don't want to see this."

The woman hesitates, glancing at me before nodding. "I'll be in the kitchen. I'll let you know if Tobias wakes up."

The enclosed space remains quiet as she leaves, the dim lighting making the atmosphere all the more sinister.

I cling to the seat beneath me, my palms sweating.

"You've got an audience now," Luca snarls. "Be careful to watch your manners in front of the lady."

"She's no lady. That right there is a filthy whore."

Luca cocks his fist and lands another punishing blow, this time to the guy's face, the *thunk* of impact loud in the small room. "You're not all that bright, are you? I suggest you make this easier on yourself and start talking."

Otis spits a glob of blood in my direction, the remnants lingering on his lower lip. "I can tell you all you like about Luther's pretty Penny. That bitch took everything he gave her and never lost a bounce in her step. She even—"

Luca lands another blow, and another, and another, as if attempting to beat away my shame with vicious force.

"Shut him down." Sebastian clenches his fists. "Make him fucking stop or I will."

The guard snickers. "Is she a sore spot? Would it make you feel better if I told you she squealed like a pig—"

My brother shoves Luca aside and grabs Otis by the throat. "You piece of shit." His arms bulge with his exerted grip. "I'll fucking kill you."

"Either control yourself or get out." Cole shoves to his feet. "*Now.*"

The air in the tight space becomes frenzied, adrenaline

and rage making it harder to breathe. Sebastian keeps choking Otis, the constriction of blood making the guard's face swell.

"Let him go." Luca claps my brother on the chest. "Let him go, Deck. Let me do my job."

My brother doesn't stop. He keeps squeezing, tighter and tighter.

"Let him go, Sebastian." The instruction is mumbled from my numb lips. It's too soon for this asshole to die. He hasn't suffered enough.

My brother glances at me, his shame and sorrow bearing down on me again. I've never hated someone's attention more. Not even predators. Or tormentors. The way my brother judges me makes my worthlessness unbearable. But he does as I ask, releasing his hold enough for Otis to gasp for breath, his coughs and splutters returning to raspy laughter.

"I'm done playing." Luca speaks to Cole. "How 'bout you?"

"Feel free to speed it up."

"No sweeter words were spoken," Luca mutters as he snatches some kind of tool from the floor—a small set of curved pruning shears. "Where are the other women, asshole? Where did Luther keep them?"

Otis smirks, exposing claret-stained teeth. "You'll never find them. Not alive."

"Have it your way." Luca walks around to the back of the chair and leans down.

I can't see what he's doing. It's the crunch, the almighty roar, the mass of splattering blood, and the lone finger that eventually falls to the floor that announces the new level of interrogation.

"I'll ask again." Luca returns to his standing position before Otis. "Where are they?"

The guard pants, his chest rising and falling as his attention turns to me. "Did you know I fucked your friends? I fucked *all* of them." He glares at me. "Luther may not have let us touch you, but we made up for it with the other bitches. They paid for your protection."

His words lash me like a whip, each injury deeper than the last.

I can't stand it. I can't sit here and take it anymore.

"Damn, Otis." Luca clucks his tongue as he returns to the back of the chair. "You're one slow motherfucker. I thought you would've learned not to mess with her by now."

There's another crunch. Another roar. Another drop of a finger to the ground.

It's not enough.

Not the tears in Otis's eyes. Not the drool blubbering from his mouth. He knows he's going to die and it's clear he won't share information no matter what's done to him. He will only continue to taunt me. To punish me.

"Chloe was the best," he slurs. "She had the tightest ass I've ever fucked."

I gasp as fury blinds me. I can't think through the need to strike. It's all I know as I push to my feet, snatch the shears from Luca's hand, and squeeze the blades together to sink the sharp depths into Otis's inner thigh.

"Burn in hell." I push the shears deeper.

He bucks, his roar ringing in my ears. There's so much noise. Shouts. Thoughts. Screams.

The past and present collide. Torture and freedom still battle in my mind.

I clutch those shears, staring Otis in the eye as strong hands wrap around my wrists and yank me backward. I can't hold on. My fingers slide from the grip, making the blades creep open while still imbedded inside flesh.

Then I'm swirled around and forced to face a brother who's ashamed of me. There's no hiding it. It's tattooed on his face.

"Let me go." I thrash. *"Let me go."*

"Fuck, Penny." Luca becomes a comforting force at my back, ushering us to the door in shuffled steps. "You need to leave."

I plant my feet, determined to stay. I have to witness the continued suffering instead of feeling it on my own.

"Don't touch me." I fling my arms, trying to loosen Sebastian's unyielding grip. "Don't ever fucking touch me."

"Get her out of here," Cole demands. *"Now."*

I wiggle. I thrash. I fight, fight, fight, but like always, I don't win.

"Let me take care of her." Luca speaks over my shoulder. "I've got this."

I drown in hysteria. Wanting and needing and suffocating.

Chloe is dead. Taylor, Anna, Emma, Ivy, Claire, Skylar, Naomi, and so many more, too.

They're all gone and I'm still here.

They're gone and I should be with them.

My legs give out beneath me as I continue to fight.

"I've got you," Luca murmurs over the madness. "It's going to be okay."

He's wrong.

So wrong, wrong, *wrong.*

I'm led from the sauna, stumbling and fumbling over my feet as a heavy hand encourages me to move faster from the low of my back.

"Keep moving." Luca guides me into the hall, then to the closest closed door. He swings it wide to drag me into the shadows.

He doesn't turn on the light. We're left in the dim hallway glow with nothing but the sound of my pounding pulse, labored breathing, and those haunting, tormenting thoughts.

"Talk to me." He begs. "What's going on in that head of yours?"

I wish I could answer, but I don't know. I don't know. *I don't know.*

I need him to make it stop—the voices, the guilt, the tightening noose.

"What the hell were you thinking, shorty?" He gets in front of me, those eyes still wild.

That I didn't want them knowing what I am. Who I am.

I don't want anyone to regret saving me. To question whether or not they wasted time or resources. And then I was thinking that maybe Otis was right. Maybe I'm a whore who asked for what I was given. That I deserved the grief of losing my friends because my lessened torture made theirs increase.

"Talk to me." He grabs my upper arms. "Let it out."

He's disappointed. Angered. And God, that feels horrible, too.

"I-I'm sorry." The words stammer over my trembling lips. "I'm sorry."

"Tell me what's going on. What's eating away at you?"

"I don't want to see him." I shake my head. I shake everywhere. "I don't want…"

"Who?" He gets closer, looking me right in the eye. "Otis?"

"Otis… Sebastian… Tobias…" I shudder, the tearless sobs congealing in my throat. "Oh, God, Toby… How am I going to tell him about Chloe? He's been through so much."

"Forget about telling him for now. We'll do it when the time is right. But you need to make me understand what's going on. I get that you wanted revenge with Otis. What I don't understand is the way you're treating your brother."

He'll never understand. And I don't know how to explain it. The words won't form.

"Do you think he betrayed you?" he asks. "Do you blame him for not finding you? Are you punishing him for being with Keira?"

Yes. Yes. *Yes.*

"It's all of that." I pull at my hair. "And none of it at the same time. I can't think. Nothing makes sense. But that look in his eye… He's judging me. He's ashamed."

"Penny, I—"

"Don't." I step away. "Don't placate me. Or belittle me. You'll never understand how he makes me weak." I wrap my arms around my waist. "Sebastian is a vulnerability I can't afford. Not when this will never be over."

"But it's already over. You're going home—"

"What home? There's nothing to return to." Hearing the truth out loud only increases my sorrow. "I can never be free. And I can't risk being around my family when I'll always have a target on my back. You should've just left me there to die."

13

___

LUCA

"This is the shock talking." I try to soothe her. "You're going to be okay."

Her suffering strips me fucking bare. I've never been sliced open by someone else's wounds before, but she does that to me. She carves. Hacks.

"You're either stupid or a liar." She retreats. "You don't know them. They're everywhere."

I follow after her. Step for step. "You didn't think I could free you from Luther, but I did. You thought I'd fail in rescuing your friends, but I did that, too. So why can't you believe me when I say you're going to be okay? I promise none of them will be left standing. I won't fucking fail."

"Then you'll die, too. Just like everyone else."

I don't know how to comfort her, but fuck, she needs comforting. And she needs to fucking realize her tormentors are all but dead. I won't let them step foot near her again.

No new scars will be inflicted over the old. There are only the lingering nightmares to face from here.

"I can't live like this, Luca." Her entire body is wracked with shudders. "I won't risk anyone else. The only person who is safe around me is Tobias because they won't touch him. Everyone else needs to stay away—Sebastian, my family. All of them. I don't want to see them ever again."

"That's not going to happen. Your family love you too much to leave you on your own."

"No. You don't understand."

"I do. I get it now." I step forward. "And what you're feeling makes sense. It's just unnecessary."

"No." She trembles. "*No.*"

"Come here." I reach out. My chest tightens, waiting for her to deny my offer of physical comfort yet the rejection never comes.

She remains immobile as I wrap my arms around her and draw her into my chest. I hold her tight as she remains rigid. I cling to her as if my hold can fix her broken pieces.

But even now she doesn't give in to weakness. There're no tears. No sobs. Just silence.

She keeps everything bottled, the powder-keg of her suffering lying under the surface, waiting to explode.

"It's going to be okay. I promise. We've all got your back," I whisper into her hair. "Trust me."

A shuffle of feet sounds near the door, making it clear someone is eavesdropping.

I expect to see Keira when a shadow passes the frame. Or maybe the kid. But when I tilt my gaze, it's Decker who stares back at me, his expression of utter devastation letting me know he overheard at least some of our conversation.

He lowers his attention from my face to my hold on his sister and with each passing second his suffering increases. "I need to speak to you."

Penny startles at his voice and shoves from my arms.

Yet again, I've taken two steps forward with her and ended up ten yards back.

"Give me a sec." I return my attention to Penny as she continues her retreat.

Those moments of comfort did diddly-dick to help her. She's still trembling, her face stricken and pale.

"Pen, I've gotta go and see what Decker wants. Will you be all right on your own for a minute?"

She doesn't respond, just keeps distancing herself from me. From help.

"Penny?" I walk after her. "Are you going to be—"

"*I'm fine.*" She raises a hand, warding off my approach. "I'm fine," she repeats softer. "I don't need you."

I'd love to say her words don't sting like a bitch, but they do. Again she's slicing me. Gashing.

"I'll be back." I stalk for the door, each step pained from the distance building between us, and enter the hall to be greeted by one temperamental motherfucker.

"How much did you hear?" I murmur under my breath.

"Enough."

"She needs help."

He scoffs. "I fucking know that. It's the person she's going to for the help that pisses me off."

"She thinks she's placing you in danger."

"I heard," he grates through clenched teeth.

"Well, did you also hear that she thinks you're judging her? That you're ashamed of what happened?"

His face transforms with fury. "Are you kidding?"

"No."

"Fucking hell." His voice echoes off the walls. "I'm not fucking judging her. I feel sorry for her. I *hurt* for her." He pounds at his chest. "But what good is that when she won't listen to me?"

I grab the sleeve of his shirt and drag him farther down the hall. "You need to sit her down and talk to her."

"I fucking wish I could, but I can't do it now." He jerks away from me. "She shortened our timeline with the guard. You need to get back in there."

"Shortened it how?"

"She stabbed him in the femoral. He's bleeding out."

Fuck. Fuck. *Fuck.*

"How much time do we have?" I start for the gym, striding out the distance.

"I don't know. I placed a tourniquet around his thigh, but it's not going to save him. We might only have minutes. An hour at most."

"How's Torian?"

"Pissed. He's sending her home."

Whiplash brings me to a stop, making Decker almost walk straight through me. "When?"

"As soon as the jet returns, she's got a one-way ticket to Portland." He shoves me forward. "Without the kid."

No, not without Tobias. That will fucking kill her.

I storm for the exercise room, needing to extinguish this fucking blaze before it builds. "Stay with her. Let me handle this."

"Me? What the hell am I going to do? She won't let me near her."

"Just watch her. Make sure she doesn't do anything

stupid." I shove open the frosted glass door, make my way through the gym, and pull open the sauna.

Cole stands before the unconscious fucker in the chair, his hands bloodied.

"Is he still alive?" I ask.

"Does it matter? He's past regaining consciousness." Torian glares at me. "He's useless to me now."

I clamp my mouth shut, well aware that the look in his eyes is born from rage. There's no reasoning with him when he's like this. There's no hope in hell.

"As soon as the jet returns, she's gone," he seethes. "Not a second longer."

Fuck me, but I nod.

I agree because I want her away from all this.

I fucking comply because the sooner she's safe back in the States, the sooner she can heal. "Let her take the kid."

His lip curls as he straightens. "No. She gets no favors from me."

"The kid isn't a favor. It's a safety concern. Let him go with her."

"No," he snarls. "He stays with me."

"You're going to risk his life by keeping him here?"

"I'm not risking anything." He takes a threatening step toward me. "I protect my family. Always have. Always will. Reinforcements are on the way. Our asses will be covered soon enough."

"That's helpful, but—"

"We're done discussing this. I'm not negotiating for her. She's too much of a fucking complication. Her ass is leaving and that's final." He bumps by me to shove from the sauna, the quick nudge to my shoulder a burning poker to my brain.

Fuck.

I stumble into the gym after him, then stop to hang my head and massage my temples, hoping the movement will help me figure out where to go from here. How to fight for her.

"Is he dead?" Keira asks.

I glance up, finding her and Decker holding open the frosted door to the hall.

"He might as well be."

"What happens now?" Decker continues forward, looking to me for guidance I don't fucking have.

"She's leaving."

He winces. "With the kid?"

"No. But maybe it's for the best. For Tobias *and* her. She's not stable enough to be his main caregiver."

"Well, good luck telling her that." He crosses his arms over his chest. "She won't take it well."

"I'm not going to be the one to tell her."

His eyes flare. "You expect it to be me? Are you fucking kidding? Seconds ago you were hugging her, but I'm the one who has to deliver the bad news? She can't even stand the sight of me."

"She's going to have to get used to it. You both are. I'm not telling her, or taking her home. That's up to you now."

"Fuck me." He wipes a hand down his face.

"Unless you'd prefer if I was the one who escorted her." It's a joke. A lame one. But for a second my chest tightens at the thought of being her savior for a little longer. It's not a role I want, though. My sights are firmly focused on taking down Luther's operation one motherfucker at a time. I made Penny a promise and I intend to keep it.

"No way in hell." He turns to the door. "I'll take care of it."

I follow him with Keira close at my back.

We reach the open doorway to the bedroom, Penny's soft sniffles sounding from inside.

"Give me some fucking space," Decker grumbles, then disappears into the room, flicking on the light and closing the door in his wake.

There's a feminine murmur of protest from inside as Keira gently grabs my arm.

"Let them have some privacy." She attempts to tug me farther along the hall.

I don't move. "In a minute."

She blinks her pretty eyes at me, soundlessly begging me to follow.

"Not now, Keira. I said I'll follow in a minute."

"He needs time alone with her. Please don't make this harder for him." She pauses, waiting for a reply. "Please, Luca, don't interrupt them." She backtracks. "I'll be waiting for you in the living room."

I ignore her as she leaves, all my senses hyper-attuned to what's going on behind that door.

Yes, I know Decker is protective of his sister. But I am, too.

I'm not going to leave her at the mercy of a situation she doesn't want, even if she's going to have to face it sooner rather than later.

I lean against the wall beside the doorframe and listen for every word.

"Stay where you are," Penny demands. "Don't come near me."

Decker sighs. "I'm not going to hurt you. How do you not know that?"

She doesn't reply.

"You're going home," he continues. "I think Cole's waiting on his jet to return from this morning. Or maybe he's calling in one that's close by, but this is all over."

I picture her gorgeous face pale with surprise. Bright eyes. Shock-parted lips. Her panic would be a tragic sight I itch to see and the temptation to take a peek eats at me.

It's the painful reminder of the remaining news that keeps me in place.

"Did you hear me?" Decker asks. "Do you understand? You're going home. You'll be able to see Mom and Dad. And God, they're going to be so fucking happy."

Shit. I should've warned him not to mention their parents.

"I don't want to see them." Her protest is growled. "You can't make me."

"It will be good for you. They can help."

"Penny?" Tobias's voice carries down the hall, his sleepy face coming into view from a bedroom up ahead. "Where is she?"

I hold a finger to my lips as he approaches, lazily blinking away sleep as the shirt I gave him hangs from his shoulders like an oversized bag.

"She's in there," I whisper. "Talking with her brother."

"Can I see her?"

"In a minute."

"*No.*" Penny raises her voice from behind the wooden door. "You're not taking me away from him. Tobias stays with me."

The little boy's eyes widen. "They're talking about

me." He lunges for the handle, determined to get inside. *"Penny?"*

For a second I consider grabbing him, using a hand around his mouth to smother his yell. It takes another split second to figure out how fucking stupid that would be. Not only because it would scare the shit out of the kid, but because there's no way Penny didn't already hear him.

"Tobias?"

The boy shoves open the door and rushes inside.

I don't follow. As much as it kills me, I remain there against the wall, giving them the privacy Keira requested.

"What's going on?" Tobias demands. "What's happening?"

"Nothing." I imagine Penny soothing him with a motherly cuddle. "My brother and I are just having a misunderstanding."

"It's not a misunderstanding, Penny. You're going home. After all this time you get to return to the people who love you the most."

"No," she yells, the pitch razoring through my head. "You're not taking me away from him. Tobias stays with me."

Silence stretches, and this time I have no trouble picturing the standoff inside that room. I can clearly see her defiance. The strong stance. The warrior expression.

"Penny, please," Decker begs. "Torian isn't going to let his brother go anywhere without him."

"Then he can return to the States with us. He can leave, too, because I won't go anywhere without Toby."

"Penny..."

"So help me God, Sebastian, if you separate us you're as good as dead to me."

Fuck.

I push from the wall and step into the open doorway. They all look at me. Three sets of eyes begging for my assistance.

"Talk to him," Penny demands. "Tell him I'm not leaving Toby."

I wish I could.

Right now, I'd give anything to make her panicked gaze soften. To relax the stiffness in a posture that must be almost crippled with exhaustion.

"It's not your brother's decision." I start toward her. "That lies with Torian, and he's not going to change his mind. Tobias needs to get to know his family. They will look after—"

"No." She shakes her head and clutches the boy's shoulders, dragging him to stand before her. "*No.*"

"Let him get to know them. Let him spend more time alone with Keira and Cole now so you can see how comfortable he is before the jet arrives."

"No." Her eyes widen, growing frantic. "I won't leave without him."

"Penny, no amount of protesting will change Cole's mind. After what you pulled with the guard, you've stamped your own ticket home. It's your choice whether you willingly walk onto the jet, or if we need to take alternate measures to get you on there safely."

Her lips part on silent words and the pained betrayal she levels on me is fucking brutal. I've gone from being her rescuer to her tormentor in the space of a few heartbeats, and I've gotta admit, the punishment is more severe than the pound in my head.

I *want* to help her. I always have. But right now, I can't

stop agreeing with Torian. She needs to get out of here. If not for safety reasons, then for her mental health. "Leaving without him will be a good thing. You can focus on yourself to start healing."

"Do *not* make decisions for me. You can't do this. You promised," she implores, clinging tighter to a boy who seems more frightened of her reaction than his future. "You said—"

"I promised to keep you safe. To protect you."

She backs herself into the wall, frantically dragging Tobias with her. "You said you wouldn't hurt me. *This* is you hurting me."

"Penny," I warn. "You're scaring the kid. I'm sure you realize the last thing you want to do is drive a wedge between him and the people who will now be taking over his care."

She swallows, her tongue frantically snaking out to swipe her lower lip. "I'm all he's got."

Somehow, deep down, I think she knows she's got the statement backward. *He's* all *she's* got. He's her hope. Her light. He's probably the only thing she has left to fight for, which makes this even harder.

"Penny, it's okay. I don't mind staying." Tobias peers up at her. "They were nice to me while you were gone. Keira told me lots of things about my family that I didn't know. I even have a niece who lives in Portland where Baba came from. But she's my age. Isn't that weird?"

The poor fucking kid is trying to console her and I'm sure she sees it.

Her wince says it all.

"She's also Luca's niece," he adds. "Luca and I share the same family."

Penny glances at me, her wince transforming to confusion before settling into more betrayal. She's judging me, disapproving of yet another connection to a crime-riddled syndicate. "You're family?"

I wish I could ignore my spike in annoyance but that fucker increases the pressure in my skull. "My brother married Torian's other sister, Layla."

She narrows her eyes. "Congratulations. Their relationship must be lucrative for you."

I don't respond, not with more than a mimicked squint.

I can be her punching bag if that's what she needs. Yeah, it fucking stings after everything I've done for her. But I get it. She's hurting.

"Tobias, why don't you let Penny have some space for a little while?" I reach out and beckon him forward. "She needs time to think."

"Penny?" The boy looks between me and the woman holding him hostage, searching for guidance from opposing sides. "What should I do?"

She drags her gaze to him, the tip of her nose turning red.

"It's okay." I keep my arm outstretched. "She's going to be right here. I just want you to get to know your family better before she leaves. It will be good for her to see you settle in."

Tobias continues ping-ponging his attention between us, raising the tension in the room. When he takes his first step away Penny's face falls, her arms wrapping around her middle as she squeezes her eyes shut.

"I'll take him." Decker reaches for the kid, placing a gentle hand on his shoulder. "Let's go see what Keira is up to."

Penny turns her back to me and faces the wall, her posture stiff as Tobias is led from the room. She doesn't cry. Or if she does, I don't hear it. There's no tremble in her shoulders. No more sniffling.

She remains strong. So fucking strong.

I don't break the silence and neither does she. I just watch her, wishing I knew how to make this easier.

"You promised," she mumbles. "You said you wouldn't hurt me, but you already have."

"This isn't me hurting you. Being sent home is a result of your actions, not mine. We needed that guard to talk and now he's useless."

"Useless?" She swings around to face me. "Why?"

"You hit an artery. He passed out from blood loss. And if he isn't already dead, he soon will be."

For a brief second, I expect her to crumple. To wither under the news. Instead, she squares her shoulders, emboldened by her increasing murder tally.

"We needed him for information. Now we're back to flying blind." I chance a step forward. "You can't blame Torian for being pissed."

"I can blame him for a whole lot of things."

I shrug. "And if it makes you feel better, go ahead. But you don't know the guy. He had no clue about his father's schemes. He didn't even know about Tobias. He might be a bit sketchy when it comes to the way he earns his money, but he's not like Luther."

"I find that hard to believe. Luther spoke to people in Portland all the time. Almost daily. They knew what was going on."

I nod. "I don't doubt that. Cole's old man packed up and left the States years ago, but he wouldn't have severed his connections. We knew he had lingering spies. His brother, Richard, was one of them."

She pulls back, the revolt minute but there all the same.

"You knew Richard?" I ask.

She clenches those arms tighter around her middle and glances away. "No, nobody can truly know someone so evil. But I've witnessed firsthand what he's capable of."

"What he *was* capable of."

Her focus returns to mine, her face slightly downcast as she stares at me through thick lashes. "Meaning?"

"Take relief in knowing he's dead. One by one, they're all going to get taken down. I won't stop until they're all gone. You can leave knowing I'm keeping my promise to end this."

She holds my stare, those dark eyes stirring up shit inside me that shouldn't be felt. Not for Decker's sister. Not for a broken, tormented beauty of a woman.

"I'm not leaving Tobias," she repeats, this time softer, without the theatrics. "I won't."

I nod, giving her a sad smile. "I wish you had a choice, shorty."

"Please, Luca." Her lips tremble. "I can't go without him."

More strikes lash my skin. Slicing deep. All I want to do is give her what she wants. Instead, I have to take solace in giving her what she needs. "You should freshen up. Take a shower and get some rest." I start for the door. "You've got another big day ahead of you."

14

PENNY

I spend a long time standing near the door, listening to the soft murmur of friendly conversation between Tobias and Keira. She makes him laugh. Despite everything he's been through, he takes to her effortlessly.

And maybe that's what he needs—happiness. The freedom to breathe without restriction from a brutal father.

I guess he also needs the positivity and bright outlook that I've only ever been able to fake. I may smother him in cuddles and kisses, but my aura has always been filled with doom and gloom.

He yearns for something I can't provide. And who am I to keep it from him?

Nobody. That's who.

The more I remain in solitude, the more my drowning emotions shift, their slow retreat making it easier to think as the hollowness returns.

Everyone is better off without me. My sisters. Toby.

I've never been helpful to any of them. I was responsible for more women suffering because of Luther's obsession with me. Once Tobias finds out, he'll hate me. And so he should. Not only for the damage I inflicted, but because I can't bring myself to tell him about Chloe.

He'll have to find out from someone else. Someone foreign.

Keira, maybe.

I push from the wall and escape into the adjoining bathroom to take the shower Luca suggested. I hang my head under the spray. I try to let the water cleanse me, but there's no escaping the exhausting weight of my failures.

I never wanted to see myself as a victim. I'd always fought. Strategized. Manipulated. I stupidly had the misunderstanding that I was beating Luther somehow. That I was trapped playing his game, but I'd figured out a way to cheat him.

Turns out they knew what I was doing and punished those I love because of it.

And now I'm so goddamn broken I can't even cry to let the turmoil escape. My tears dried years ago, probably never to be seen again.

When the water turns my skin to wrinkles, I shut off the taps and dry myself, reclaiming the dress made from material that harbors a lifetime of unwanted memories. I've been choked in this dress. Gagged.

I have no energy anymore. No determination. I'm done.

There's nothing left to do but crawl into the crisp bed and pray for the peace of sleep that doesn't bless me for a long time. I doze briefly, my consciousness fading in and out until Tobias crawls onto the mattress in front of me to spoon against my chest.

"I'm sorry. I didn't mean to wake you." He nestles closer, not protesting when I wrap my arms around him.

"It's okay. I'm glad you did." I nuzzle my face into the back of his neck. "How was your time with Keira?"

"She's nice." He snuggles in tight, his warmth enveloping me. "We had more cookies and hot chocolate. And she told me how Sebastian always steals her favorite thin mints or hides them from her. I don't know what thin mints are but she said she'll buy me some when we get to her house."

"Her house?" My heart pangs, my entire body protesting his speedy connection to his half-sister.

"She lives in Portland." He yawns. "It's in Oregon. You know, where Baba was from? She says I can come live with her for a little while. Or with her sister and my niece. She said I get to choose. Where do you think we should stay?"

We.

He asks with such naive simplicity. As if I'll be with him, our futures entwined when I'm not sure they will even brush. "Why don't you decide?"

"Are you sure?" He pauses. "What's wrong? You seem sad."

I shake my head and refuse to sniff away the tingle in my nose. "I'm tired, that's all."

I'm sure if he was older he'd be able to see through the thinly veiled placation. My barely restrained resentment of Keira, too. He's slipping through my fingers so fast. I almost can't believe how easily he's taken to his new family, until I acknowledge the iron fist he's lived with since birth.

"I'm tired, too." He wiggles, bumping into me. "You can help me decide in the morning."

"I'm leaving soon, Tobias. You understand that, right?"

"Mmm." He nods into me. "You're going to America and I need to stay here with Keira and Cole. But it's only for a little while. Just like a sleepover."

I press my lips into his hair and close my eyes. "Yeah. Just like a sleepover."

There're moments of silence, the nothingness stretching into agonizing heartbeats. I want to cling to him. To squeeze so tight. But I refuse to let him see me suffer. He's already been through enough.

"You're not going to miss Baba, are you?" He turns toward me to stare through the darkness. "Not even a little bit?"

"No," I answer honestly. "I won't."

"I don't want to miss him either," he whispers. "But I do."

"Oh, sweetheart, it's okay to feel that way. You're allowed to miss him, and you're allowed to want to forget him, too. It's even okay to miss him one minute and want to forget him the next. There's no rules for grief."

"Grief?"

I give a half-hearted smile. "It's an adult word to describe the mix of feelings we have when someone dies."

"I don't like grief. It hurts."

"Yes, it does. But it gets easier with time." Or so I'm told.

"Keira lost her baba today, too. Do you think she knows he was a bad man?"

I exhale a heavy breath, not feeling comfortable answering anything where Keira is concerned. "I think she only found out recently. But maybe that's something the two of you can discuss. You can tell her what it was like to live with your father, just like she's telling you what it will be like to live with her in Portland."

He pulls back, pausing a moment. "I can tell her things? I wasn't sure I was allowed."

"Yes, you can tell her." It's time for me to give up my parental hold. Once I'm gone, I'm sure they'll never let me back into his life. I'll be a stranger. A fading memory.

"Do you think she's like him?"

My insides squeeze, my conscience preparing to wage war with my insecurities. "I think if she was like him you wouldn't feel comfortable around her. You're a smart boy, Toby. Listen to what your heart tells you."

"My heart tells me I'm going to miss you."

I struggle to breathe as I pull him into me, placing a punishing kiss to his forehead. "I'm going to miss you like crazy, little man."

"Keira said you would." He wraps an arm around my waist. "She also said you need to go home and be with your family. That they're the ones who will make all this better."

I don't appreciate her spinning those lies. I also don't appreciate her making this easier on him. That's meant to be my job. Yet I'm struggling to do it.

"That's right. Everything will be better once I'm home." I give him a quick squeeze, then drag my arm back to my side. "But now it's time for you to get some rest."

"Okay." He sighs, swiveling around so his back faces me again. "Good night."

"Good night, little man."

I stay there in the quiet while his breathing grows shallow. Peaceful. He doesn't twitch or cry out. For a long time, I wait for nightmares to plague him but when they never come I slide from the bed, too overtired to sleep.

I walk from the room and into the dimly lit hall. I don't hear chattering voices anymore. There's nothing. No sound.

I wonder if the guard is still in the sauna, his blood covering the floor, my crime readily available for anyone to see.

I question whether Torian will dispose of the evidence like he did with Chris. Will the body disappear? Will the scent of bleach fill the sauna the same way it does in the living room? Or will his body remain there, waiting to be found with my fingerprints on the shears?

I continue strolling through the house aimlessly. I reach the frosted door to the gym, then think better of returning to that nightmare. Instead, I turn to retrace my steps. I walk by a closed door with murmuring voices emanating from the other side—Keira and my brother. I keep going, keep passing rooms until I'm at the most familiar, standing in front of Luca's ajar door, the slight opening to the awaiting darkness taunting me to take a look.

I don't fight the desire. I'm done fighting all together.

I sneak inside to find him outstretched on the bed, the light from the hall casting him in a faint glow as one arm rests over his eyes. He's shirtless, his satin boxers the only thing covering a partial part of the landscape of dips and dives built of muscle and sinew.

I don't know why, but an invisible string pulls me forward. I can't stop the momentum.

Before—at the start—I hated him for the way he tempted my hope. Now I want to apologize for what I've put him through. He's done so much. Too much.

I continue my silent approach to the foot of his bed and watch him sleep, his inhales long and drawn, the exhales smooth and subtle.

I shouldn't be here. Shouldn't remain staring at him, the quiet minutes making him more familiar. But I'm caught up noticing the smaller details I hadn't noticed earlier. I see the stubble on his face, which is now longer than when we first met. He's more rugged. More ragged. Then there's his mouth, and those lips that appear far kinder when they're not pressed tight with disappointment.

"Can I help you?" he mumbles.

I gasp, my heart squeezing as I grasp at my chest. "I-I didn't mean to wake you."

He remains still, that muscled arm continuing to shield his face. "I haven't slept."

"Not at all?" I blurt. "You should've said something."

He lowers his arm, his dark eyes capturing mine. "I was waiting to see if you were going to try to kill me again. Then I began hoping you would because my head is fucking killing me."

I wince, wishing my gratitude over him saving me was enough to stop his pain. "I'll go." I backtrack. "I'm sorry for disturbing you."

"No. Stay." He places his hands behind his head, his brow pinching as he re-settles himself on the pillow. "What's on your mind?"

Nothing.

Everything.

I don't even know where to start.

"Can't sleep?" he asks.

"Not really." I lower my gaze to the bedframe and rest my fingers on the carved wood. "I think I'm too tired."

"Tell me what's worrying you." He sits higher, still wincing with the movement when he rests against the headboard.

He sounds sincere. So real. So caring.

I hate it and love it at the same time.

"What will happen to my sisters?" I divert the conversation away from me. "What will Hunter do with them once they land?"

"They'll be taken somewhere to regroup for a while. A safe house of sorts. That's where they'll be coached on what to say to their family and the authorities once they're ready to return home."

"But they definitely get to go home, right?"

"Of course."

"And what about me? Will I go through the same process?"

He shrugs. "Something similar, I assume. But that's up to Sebastian."

My pulse quickens. "Why him? Why does he get to decide?"

His lips part, his hesitation speaking volumes.

"Luca?"

"You weren't told he's the one taking you home?"

"No, I wasn't." I guess I should've expected it, yet here I am, surprised and beating away panic. "I could go on my own. I don't need him to take me."

"You'd leave an island where you were enslaved, with no protection, to board a jet with pilots you don't know, all because you don't want to be near your brother?"

"I told you why—"

"I know." He raises a dismissive hand. "I get it. But I'm not going to let you leave alone. It's not safe."

I wish he wasn't right. I wish so badly, because that flight will be hell.

"Have you allowed yourself to grieve yet?" he asks.

"I haven't stopped grieving since Luther stole my life."

He nods, the movement slight. "Want to talk about it?"

"No." Not the violations or the punishments.

"What about Chloe? Do you want to talk about her?" He stares at me, his comfort sinking into my heart. "How long did you know her?"

"Six months. Maybe a little more."

I remember the day she arrived, her face red and swollen, her cheek blackened with a hearty bruise. Some women took their time opening up to the other members of Luther's harem, but not Chloe. She fell into my arms at first sight and cried for hours.

"What will happen to her body?"

He sucks in a tired breath. "Honestly, I don't know."

"Please don't lie to me."

"I assure you, I have no idea." He rakes a hand through the unscathed side of his head, ruffling his hair. "I haven't discussed it with Torian. But if I had to take a guess, I'm confident you wouldn't be comforted by the answer."

I thought as much.

Her body will disappear just like Chris and Luther's. There won't be a funeral. Or a memorial for a woman who deserved so much more than the world gave her.

"I'm sorry," he murmurs. "I wish you weren't going through this."

I lower my gaze to the bed as I battle the effects of his

sympathy. I haven't experienced kindness in a long time. Especially not from a man.

"Is there anything I can do?" he asks.

I could reiterate how much I want to stay. That separating me from Tobias is only going to make my life harder, but the quiet hours alone have made me realize that he'll be fine without me. It's better for him if he doesn't witness any of my upcoming meltdowns.

"I think you've done enough." I glance up at him through my lashes, our gazes brushing.

"I haven't done anything."

"Yes, you have. And I want to thank you for it all. I wish I could repay you."

"You can."

My heart stops, and for a brief moment I dive back into the heavy ocean of fear as I wait for him to request sexual favors.

"You can get help," he whispers. "Do whatever it takes to reclaim your life and be happy again."

A relieved breath escapes me. He keeps proving he's not like the others. But I return my attention to the covers, not wanting to lower myself to explain why his request is impossible. Can someone without worth find happiness? Is it even possible?

"You're important, Penny—you know that, right?" He pauses, the silence killing me softly. "Your life has meaning and value. People love you."

My eyes burn as he strips me layer by layer. Word by word.

"And if there's anything else you need from me, I'll give it to you," he continues. "Even if it means laying here in silence, pretending I'm asleep, while you try to figure me out."

"I don't need to figure you out. I'm leaving, remember?" I shoot him a glance.

"How could I forget?" He grins. "I'm devastated that I'm losing the one person who can keep me on my toes."

"Don't worry. Tobias will fill those shoes quick enough."

He chuckles, the sound husky and low. All his tenderness flows into me, the effect punishing. A raging flood after a lifetime of drought. "Is anything else worrying you?"

How does he know? How can he read me so easily? "You said one of the guards escaped. Doesn't that mean it's not safe here?"

"It's safe enough." He holds my gaze, his confidence reassuring. "We can hear anyone approach. And there are already mercenaries out on the water keeping watch. Soon, Torian will have this place locked tighter than Fort Knox. Then there's Hunter, too. He'll return as soon as he hands over your friends."

"Hands them over to who?"

"My brother."

I nod, slightly comforted by his answer. If his brother is even half the man Luca is, I'm almost convinced my sisters will be in good hands. "And what about you?"

"What about me?"

"Will you get help? Will you see a doctor? I don't think someone in your condition should even be sleeping unsupervised."

His lips kick. "Are you offering to keep watch, shorty?"

There's a beat of silence where I blink in shock at the unexpected flirtation.

"Fuck," he curses under his breath. "I didn't mean to…"

"It's okay." I shake my head, my cheeks heating.

"No. I'm fucking sorry," he grates. "I didn't mean anything by it."

"I know." I truly believe him, because why would a man like him flirt with a whore like me? It was clearly a mistake. "You don't need to explain."

A door opens directly across the hall and Cole steps out, his scrutinizing attention falling on me before coming to rest on Luca.

He raises a brow, drawing assumptions about my presence before he clears his throat. "The jet is here. It's time to leave."

I beat back the burst of apprehension and retreat from the end of the bed. "Am I allowed a few moments to see Tobias one last time? I won't wake him."

Cole gives a short nod, his face remaining tight.

"Thank you." I hate those words. I hate that I'm giving them to him. But they're necessary. He cleaned up one of my murder victims and I desperately need him to clean up the second.

I turn back to Luca. "Thank you again. For everything."

"Don't mention it."

I don't wait for the discomfort of this farewell to set in. Once I leave here, I won't think of my harsh protector again. I can't. People like Luca are only a temporary fantasy.

I hustle from his bedroom and make my way to Tobias,

my heart squeezing at the sight of him resting peacefully in the single bed. I make sure not to get too close and remain hovering at the door, the brush of light footsteps approaching seconds later.

"Cole said you're leaving." Keira comes to stand beside me.

I nod, not dragging my attention from Toby.

"You're not waking him?" she queries.

"No." As selfish as it is, I'm going to leave without saying goodbye. He doesn't need to witness my theatrics. The poor kid has already been through enough without having to deal with whatever direction my unpredictable emotions decide to take.

"All he does is speak about you," she continues. "He said you're like a mother to him."

My eyes blaze, the promise of tears hovering close, yet so far.

"You can call him any time." She keeps her voice low. "You can video chat and email or text. Whatever you like."

"I don't have a phone."

"I'll make sure you get one. And if there's anything else, you only need to ask Sebastian. He'll get it for you."

With dirty money, no doubt, but I keep that thought to myself.

"Did Luca tell you how your brother came to be a part of our family?" She leans against the doorjamb, her body turned toward me.

"No, and I don't want to hear it. I'm not ready."

"I understand. But if you ever need someone to talk to, I'm always—"

"Keira." I turn to her. "I appreciate the offer, but I can whole-heartedly tell you I will never, *ever* seek out the daughter of my rapist as a comforting shoulder. I'm sure you can understand that, too."

She holds my gaze, her pained eyes punishing me. "Yes, I do."

"Thank you." I walk into the room to kneel before the bed. I place my hands on the edge of the mattress and my chin atop them to stare at Tobias.

"Is there anything I should know about him?" Keira inches toward me. "Any medical history or useful information?"

There's seven years worth of things she should know. All his demons. All the damage. But maybe those ghosts are better left buried until Tobias is ready for the outside world to know.

"He's allergic to grass," I whisper. "It's nothing serious. He'll break out in bumps all over his skin and he'll itch like crazy. Just make sure you put him in a bath and give him an antihistamine."

"Okay. I can do that."

"And he doesn't like carrots." My throat clogs as I recount memories of our time together. "At all. No matter what they're mixed with, he won't eat them."

She lets out a breath of a chuckle. "Stella's the same with corn."

"And don't listen to him if it gets to bedtime and he says he's not tired. He always is, and it's ten times harder to get him to sleep if you give in."

I can't remember how many nights he's talked me into staying awake an extra thirty minutes, only to throw an unruly tantrum when it finally came time to crawl into bed.

The kid has always been a master manipulator. At least

where my heart was concerned. He knew he could talk me into anything if he tried hard enough. Usually, all it took was a bat of those innocent eyes and a pout of his kiddy lips.

"What time?" Keira asks.

"Excuse me?" I glance at her, confused by the question.

"What time should he go to bed?"

"Oh." I frown. "He'll be thrown out of whack because of the last two days. But usually he's in bed by eight-thirty. A little later on weekends if he promises to sleep in."

I turn back to him and reach out, sliding a lock of hair from his face. "I'm going to miss you, little man," I whisper, my throat tightening.

He whimpers, his eyes still closed when he says, "Penny?"

"Go back to sleep, sweetheart."

He nuzzles into his pillow and lets out a sigh. "Are you leaving?" His question comes so easily as he remains in sleep mode.

"Yes. I need to get to the airport."

He nods. "Keira says I can call you whenever I want."

"That's right. Whenever you like. No matter what time it is."

He nods again, his face remaining nestled against the pillow. He doesn't say another word. As far as I know, he's slipped back into sleep.

Again, so easily.

Without a care.

I lean in, place the lightest kiss to his cheek and begin to drag myself away, only to have him wrap an arm around my neck, holding me tight.

I smile through the heartache. I fucking die through it.

"I love you," he murmurs.

I close my eyes, pressing my forehead to his cheek. "I love you, too. I love you more than anything."

I remain against him for a tortured eternity, his hold slowly loosening, his breathing returning to the deep lull of slumber.

When he starts to let out the lightest rumble of a snore, I break away, gently guiding his arm to the mattress.

Each retreating step is done not only with reluctance, but with soul-tearing sadness. And when I turn to face Keira, she's not there, Luca having taken her place in the doorway.

He's dressed, in black jeans and a matching T-shirt, and with the growing stubble along his jaw, the mass of darkness makes his hazel eyes more intense.

"Are you ready?" he asks.

"Do I have a choice?

"Nope."

I sigh. "Then yes, I'm ready."

"Keira will take good care of him. She's always been great with kids. And I'll keep an eye on him, too."

"Thank you."

I follow him as he leads the way down the hall and into the living room. My brother is already there, leaned against the back of a sofa, a suitcase at his side, his gaze lowered. He doesn't look up as I approach. The only acknowledgement of my existence comes from the slight tightening of his shoulders. The lightest flinch.

"Well, I'll see you around, shorty." Luca gives my shoulder a quick squeeze, the touch lingering well after he drags his hand away. "Look after your—"

"I wouldn't say your farewells just yet." Torian pushes

from his seat at the dining table to walk toward us. "You're the one taking her home."

There's an awkward pause. My stomach drops. Everyone glances at each other. Me to Luca. Luca to Sebastian. Sebastian to Cole.

"No, he's not." My brother straightens from the sofa. "I am."

"You were," Torian corrects. "But not anymore. It's Luca who has to leave."

15

———

LUCA

"No fucking way," Decker snarls. "I'm taking her back. Not him."

"There's been a change of plan." Torian pins me with a stare. "You need to return to Portland."

"Why?" Foreboding crawls up my spine. He's got that look in his eyes again. The one that announces he's made up his mind. "What happened?"

"You're hurt. It's not safe for anyone if you stay."

"Then give him some Advil and a fuckin' Band-Aid and he'll be fine." Decker clenches his fists at his sides, barely containing his anger. "Because she's not leaving with him."

"I'm not arguing over this. Luca is injured, so he's the one getting out of here."

"I'm not injured, Torian. I'm good." I might feel like I'm suffering the worst hangover of my existence, my eyes seemingly coated in a thin layer of gravel while my head continues to pound. But essentially, I'm good. "It's a fucking scratch."

"A scratch?" He approaches, his smile dark as he shoves my chest.

"*Fuck.*" I stumble backward, my skull clenching as if it's in a vise. "What the fuck was that for?"

Torian takes a swing, confusing the hell out of me.

I duck and lose my balance. I stumble, fumbling over my feet, my vision darkening as I land on my fucking ass. Hard.

"You're good?" Torian stands over me, looking down his nose at my fucked-up position on the floor. "Really? You can't even stay on your feet, which means you're far from good. You're a fucking liability."

"He's got a concussion." Penny rushes toward me, her eyes filled with concern as she offers a hand to help me stand. "Are you all right?"

"Don't." I bat away her offer and shove to my feet. "I'm not a fucking invalid. And I'm not going back with her." I shoot her a sideways glance of apology and feel like an absolute prick for the wince plastered across her face. "No offence, shorty, but my place is here. I earned the right to take down those assholes. I'm not leaving until it's done."

"You're injured," Torian repeats.

"Yeah, well, I'm no fucking doctor but putting me on a jet while concussed doesn't seem like a brilliant idea either."

"If you stay, you're a distraction and I've already got enough of those. So go home. Rest up. And if we're still here once you get back on your feet you can return."

"I can rest here," I snarl. "Decker's the one who wants to take her home."

"If Deck goes, it leaves Keira and Tobias without trustworthy protection. I may be paying those mercenaries by the truckload, but I need someone on the inside I can rely on."

Fuck him. Fuck this. "I was reliable last night. I led the entire fucking operation at your father's house."

"It wasn't my brother or sister's lives you were risking on that mission. And at the time, I was too caught up in my own head to realize how bad your injuries were."

"This is ridiculous." I scoff. "Why can't you get Keira to take her back?"

"I fucking agree," Decker snaps. "Let Keira do it."

"No, she stays to look after the kid." He walks away. "I'm not arguing over this. My mind is already made up. Safe travels."

I follow him, stalking two steps behind as we enter the secluded hall. "And what the fuck am I meant to do with her once we get to Portland? As it is, my brother can barely handle the responsibility of one woman, but you've lumped him with three fucking fragile victims. You expect him to take on a fourth?"

"No, I expect you to take care of it."

"Torian," I warn. "Stop fucking with me."

"I'm not fucking with you." He turns to face me. "And I'll never forget what you've done here. You've gone above and beyond for my family. It's a debt I hope to one day repay, which is why I'm starting right now by looking after you seeing as though you don't want to do it yourself."

"I'm fine." I launch my fist at the wall, my knuckles breaking plaster, pain shooting to my head. I need to stay here to make those fuckers pay. To make sure any other women are freed. To get Penny her revenge.

Torian raises a brow. "A few short days ago, you were

bragging that your macho ex-SEAL ass could kick mine without effort. Now you're falling on that ass after I throw an air swing. So forgive me for relying on my own judgment to make this call." He claps me on the shoulder, hard. I'm sure it's in an effort to increase the pounding in my head. "Keep me updated. I'll see you in a while."

He continues down the hall, ending the conversation with a definitive slam of his door. *Again,* I'm sure it's just to trigger my migraine.

Fuck.

I slump against the wall.

I'd been apprehensive at the thought of entrusting someone else with Penny's safety. I'd even contemplated being the one to take her home. Now the reality is so fucking far from comforting it's almost scary.

I'm not the one who should be looking after her. Not after I slipped subtle flirtation into our conversation. And that isn't the worst of it. Those words hold no comparison to my thoughts. My fucking obsession.

She shouldn't be around me.

And I definitely shouldn't be entrusted with her.

I rest the back of my head against the wall, not moving when Decker enters the hall to storm toward me.

"Don't start," I warn. "I don't want to hear it."

"Too fucking bad." He stands in front of me, chest puffed, shoulders stiff. "Every time I take a breath you're getting closer and closer to my sister."

"Not by choice."

"I don't give a shit if it's by choice, or circumstance, or divine fucking intervention. If you so much as make her sniffle, I'll fucking destroy you."

I take his fury. Mainly because I don't have the mental

capacity to retaliate, but also because I'd be equally bitter if the situation was reversed.

"Keep her safe. Keep her happy. Or I'll..." He pauses, his hostility ebbing as he diverts his focus blankly down the hall. "Just keep her fucking safe, okay?"

"I will," I vow, then hang my head, despising how this is really fucking happening. And after the bullshit I went through with Luther. The risks I took to take him down. The bullets I dodged. And the one I caught with my thick skull.

"I can go on my own," Penny's fortified voice carries from the entrance to the living room. "Nobody needs to escort me."

I don't answer her. Don't even look.

Neither does Decker. All he does is glare. At me. Like this is all my fucking fault.

"If someone can get me to the jet, I'll make it back by myself. It's no big deal."

"You're not going on your own." I push from the wall and sidestep her brother to continue toward her. "What's done is done. There's no changing Torian's mind."

"But you want to stay. And I don't need a bodyguard."

"It doesn't matter—"

"Yes, it does." She stands her ground, reclaiming her warrior status, not letting me pass into the living room. "I won't take this from you."

It's in those words that I realize my protests are truly pathetic.

The day Luther died she told me something that stuck with me. Something I despised.

She implied she was a possession. Explained that she was a gift.

It's now that I realize no truer words were ever spoken. She *is* a gift. And it should be considered an honor to accompany her home.

"You're not taking anything from me, shorty." I stare into those dark eyes and wish I didn't feel a thrum of connection. No, not a thrum—a fucking avalanche. "I'm being sent back because of my head and there's nothing I can do about that. My issue revolves around the promise I made to you. I told you I'd clean house with Luther's men, and I don't go back on my word."

"Will they still be taken down?"

"Yes," Sebastian answers for me. "Without a doubt."

She sucks in a breath and raises her chin. "Then you're not going back on your word. You're just letting someone else take care of it. Maybe that's for the best. Like Torian said, you need to rest."

"There's not going to be a lot of rest when I've got you to contend with." I wink at her, trying to ease the tension. "Somehow I think you're going to make it hard to keep you out of trouble."

She releases a rasp of a laugh, her smile slight as she lowers her gaze to the floor. Shy. Almost submissive.

Fuck, she's beautiful.

Breathtaking.

Tempting.

Trouble is definitely going to be on my radar. And there's no way her protection will ever take a back seat to my recovery.

But it's no longer Luther or his guards I have to keep her safe from.

The biggest threat to her right now is me.

· · ·

TO BE CONTINUED...

Please consider leaving a review on your book retailer
website or Goodreads

Titles in the Hunting Her Series

Hunter

Decker

Torian

Savior

Luca

Cole

**Information on Eden's other books can be found at
www.edensummers.com**

ABOUT THE AUTHOR

Eden Summers is a bestselling author of contemporary romance with a side of sizzle and sarcasm.

She lives in Australia with a young family who are well aware she's circling the drain of insanity.
Eden can't resist alpha dominance, dark features and sarcasm in her fictional heroes and loves a strong heroine who knows when to bite her tongue but also serves retribution with a feminine smile on her face.

If you'd like access to exclusive information and giveaways, join Eden Summers' newsletter via the link on her website - www.edensummers.com

For more information:
www.edensummers.com
eden@edensummers.com